The Laugh Peddler

The Laugh Peddler

A STORY BY

Alice E. Christgau

ILLUSTRATED BY

Arvis L. Stewart

Young Scott Books, New York

OTHER BOOKS BY
Alice E. Christgau

Runaway to Glory
Rosabel's Secret

for JACK *and* TIM

Library of Congress Catalog Card No. 68-15340
Text © 1968 by Alice E. Christgau. Illustrations © 1968 by Arvis L. Stewart

Contents

1. The Coming of the Peddler

Late in the afternoon of a dreary November day, Sidney and Elizabeth stood at the kitchen windows looking out at the sleety rain. It had begun falling as they walked home from district school and was steadily growing heavier.

The farmhouse kitchen was warm and pleasant. Mama stepped around briskly preparing supper, and the three-year-old twins, Ernest and Ellen, sat placidly in their high chairs munching apples. Yet the two older children stared out discontentedly. Usually when they came home from school and finished their small chores, they were allowed to go outside to play, taking the twins along. But today, because of the weather, Mama said firmly that there would be no going out except for the most necessary reasons.

"Go out in such weather?" she scolded. "Absolutely not! It's getting colder, too. This rain will turn to snow—see if it doesn't. We'll have early winter, and we're not at all ready for it."

"We could play in the barn," hopefully offered Elizabeth.

But Mama said "No" with finality. "You'd get soaked just going out there. This once you can stay in—and here's something you can do. Try to spot my good wool quilt in the yard. I can't understand what happened to it. When I went to take the bedding in from airing last night, that quilt was gone. It might have blown off the line and Doogan dragged it off, but he's too old for such tricks now. If it gets wet through it will be ruined. See if you can't spot a bit of color from the windows there."

The children stood looking in all directions, but saw no bright color anywhere. There were only the dull tans, grays, and browns of the stubbly cornfield and the near-black of the plowed grain fields, with the dark green accent from the fir trees in the grove. Even the little patch of lake that could be glimpsed through a corner of the one window was gray, for the water had begun to freeze over a few days before.

Sidney, who was small for his twelve years, stood stretching, trying to reach the top of the window frame. He had heard that if you stretched a lot you would grow faster, and he was anxious to grow. As it was, he was the same size as Elizabeth, who was younger by a whole year.

His blue-gray eyes seemed too big in his small face; they

* 8 *

looked out questioningly from a shock of cornhusk-tan hair and changed from gray to blue, depending on the state of his emotions. Most often they were gray.

Size was the only similarity between the two children, though they were first cousins. Sidney was the orphan son of Mama's sister and had lived with the Millers since he had lost both his parents within one month right after Christmas last year. He was already dreading the approach of the 1914 Christmas.

Sometimes just before falling asleep at night, he would remember that sad time when grief piled upon grief had numbed him into shivering coldness. First had come his father's death, following an operation too long delayed. Then four weeks later—after he had kept reassuring his little sister Mabel that "Mummy will soon get better"—his mother also died from pneumonia, after an ordinary cold that would not get better. He still stiffened with terror at times, remembering that day afterwards when he heard the neighbors, who had taken him into their cramped little apartment, talking in the kitchen. "What's to become of the boy?" said Mrs. Moe to her husband. "No one seems to want him," was the answer. "Well, it's a good thing there are places for such kids."

There was no money left at all and, though golden-haired little Mabel was quickly spoken for by his father's relatives in the East, there wasn't anyone who wanted him even temporarily. Sidney knew that what Mr. Moe called "places" meant just one thing—the orphanage.

And then this Aunt Matilda—whom he'd never even seen except in a picture—appeared, just in time for his mother's funeral. Sidney found immediate comfort in her nearness, if only because she looked a little like his mother and had some of her soft ways. He felt the numbness thaw a little as she helped him pack his things to take along home.

He knew that her appearance saved him from the orphanage, for she had told him right away that she was taking him home with her. He was to live with her and Uncle Fred on their Minnesota farm and be brought up as one of their own children. "You'll like living on a farm," she said. He made up his mind that he would.

It had been such a relief just to have some place to go! He knew that only unwanted children went to an orphanage, and he was familiar with the nearest one in Chicago. It was an ugly gray stucco building with two stone lions on its steps. Many times he had observed the forlorn looking orphans playing behind the iron fence and had felt vaguely sorry for them as he walked by with one or both of his parents on the way to the park. Even an unfamiliar farm and a family he had never seen was better than having to go to an orphanage.

But the adjustment had not been easy. Now ten months later, he still felt like an outsider, not really sure he belonged in the busy farm household.

He found it quite easy to call his Aunt Matilda "Mama" as the other children did. She was always so much busier than his own mother had been, but she was warm and kind.

The Coming of the Peddler

It was different with his Uncle Fred—Papa. Somehow he still stumbled trying to say that word; if he used it at all in referring to his new father, it came out a timid, hesitant "Pa."

He had felt from the first that he did not please his Uncle Fred, that the impatience and general disappointment Pa often showed was somehow his fault. He knew he was of little use on the farm, and there was always so much work to be done and never enough hands to do it. In the first weeks after he came, Pa had tried to teach him some farm chores like milking cows, but Sidney just couldn't seem to get the hang of it. The cows refused to let down their milk to his timid squeezing, and it terrified him to sit close to the kicking legs and flailing tails.

After a few tries, Pa gave up in disgust and just left him alone. Sidney helped Elizabeth with household chores, like bringing in wood and water, but he hated the feeling of having failed at more necessary kinds of farm work. Even Karl, Papa's cousin who was the hired man, helped to impress him with a feeling of uselessness.

But Elizabeth was different. She had accepted him from the first as if he were an older brother. Because he had come from a big city—an exciting place she did not know at all—she regarded him as a bit superior. She trusted his judgment, feeling that his experience was much broader than her own. They had a good companionable relationship, and it helped Sidney to know that he was important to one person.

Elizabeth's brown braids were tied with faded red ribbons. Her face was full and rosy, and her blue eyes wide and bright. She stood on sturdy legs beside Sidney, pressing her nose against the window pane.

With Christmas approaching, their thoughts and conversation centered on the question of gifts. They had begun the subject after parting with Larry Larsen at his turn-off road. Sidney had remembered Christmas in Chicago.

"I know it can't be the same here," he had said earnestly. He did not want Elizabeth to think him ungrateful. "Farmers always have to work so hard and never seem to have much money to spend. But I can't help remembering how Christmas was when Daddy and Mummy—when we were all together. When I was little, I'd get things like tin soldiers and drums; then later I got a wagon and skates. Mabel and I always hung up our stockings and they'd be filled with candy and all the little stuff, you know. Even though Daddy wasn't feeling well last year, we still got some presents. And our dinner was very good, too."

His face became animated, but he paused as Elizabeth remained silent, adding softly, "It was a good Christmas."

They plodded on silently for a while until Elizabeth spoke. "Papa and Mama give us useful things like clothes we need, and mittens and caps—stuff like that. It isn't easy when you have to pay for a farm with what you raise, and then sometimes—like this year—you lose most of your crops." They had been dangerously close to a quarrel, and recognizing this, they dropped the subject.

The Coming of the Peddler

But now, standing at the windows, with Mama out of hearing in the pantry, Elizabeth brought it up again. "If only I had some money so I could get Mama a present! I have about fifty cents left of my birthday dollar, and I can't think of any way to get more. Oh but things are dreary this year!"

"I'd like to give her something nice too," Sidney answered. "She's been so good to me—almost like—" He looked suddenly sad, but continued quickly, "I have only about a quarter myself, but there must be a way to get more. That Larry! Bragging about the fancy locket and chain he bought for his mother in Minneapolis! It's easy for him to have money, with a rich uncle who pays him for every little bit of work he does over at his place. But don't worry," he finished hastily as the pantry door opened, "I'm sure I'll think of something."

"I can't see the quilt anywhere," said Elizabeth.

"If that isn't the strangest thing," said Mama. "There wasn't even a wind last night. Where could it have gone?"

"Maybe Doogan dragged it down to the lake pasture," Sidney suggested. "We can't see that from here, but I could put on rubbers and go look for it there."

Suddenly he peered up the lane road. "Someone's coming," he announced. "Walking in the rain like anything. He's turning into our road, too!"

A figure had appeared over the rise where the big road joined their own little road. It plodded past the mailbox and came on toward the house. In another moment Sidney cried out, "I know who it is! It's the Laugh Peddler!"

The faces in the kitchen suddenly brightened. The twins

began to pound their high chairs with fat fists, and Mama, glancing hastily in the mirror, smoothed her hair.

"I was just wondering if he wouldn't be around one of these days," she said. She shook up the stove and put in another stick of wood, then cleared a litter of apple peelings from the table and filled the tea kettle.

The figure was easily recognizable now. Only a foot peddler had that particular kind of hump on his back. It was made by a heavy pack strapped across his shoulders.

Sidney had first met him last spring on a day when he had been feeling especially forlorn. He remembered the exciting conversations he'd had with the strange man, whose like he had never known existed. In Chicago the things one needed were bought in the big stores, but here was a human walking store!

From that one visit, Sidney already knew what wonders that big pack contained. It was a suitcase, unlike ordinary suitcases, consisting of a stout leather box with a box-like cover that lifted off when it was unstrapped. The peddler always referred to it as "my portmanteau," and it was filled with all sorts of things that he hoped to sell to the housewives along his peddling route. This was his way of making a living, not an unusual one in the early 1900's when towns were small and the western half of the country sparsely settled.

Peddlers traveled between farm homes in rural areas and brought to farm wives a variety of things that they could not easily get except in the bigger stores. The more prosperous ones traveled with horse and wagon; others went on foot,

carrying their packs on their backs. The Farmers' Company Store in town, with its limited lines of merchandise, was the only shopping place most farm families had. Automobiles were not yet in common use, and trips to the city were not often made.

But Yusef Hanna, commonly known as the Laugh Peddler, came through twice a year—in the spring and fall. He was a familiar figure in the area, as this had been his territory for years. He sold a few lengths of dress cloth, table linens, towels, scarves, laces, thread, ribbon, buttons, needles—even a few trinkets and pieces of jewelry. In the heat of the summer and after the snow came in winter he "laid up" as he called it, staying at home in St. Paul and working at odd jobs. But when the weather was good, he strapped on his pack and took to the road.

Now here he was, bowing and smiling on their doorstep as Mama opened the door to his knock. Removing his rubbers and rain cape, he looked around the cozy kitchen appreciatively. Then sweeping off his cap with a flourish, he greeted them.

"Well, hullo everybody! Ah, I see you were waiting for me!" He shook hands with Mrs. Miller, and with a quick shrugging movement slipped off his heavy pack.

"But you're all looking a little sober, seems like." He glanced around at the children and gave their mother a wink. "Ah, the weather, eh? Have to stay in, and that's hard when you're full of life. I guess you're needing to buy a few laughs again. My supplies are kind of low this time of year—but

don't worry; I have a few left. All kinds, too." He patted
the bulging portmanteau importantly. "They come in sizes
to fit everybody."

A long black mustache swept across his swarthy cheeks,
but it could not hide the warmth of his full, round face. His
brown eyes contrasted sharply with their own blues and
grays, not only in color, but in the dancing lights shining in
their depths.

They sparkled now as he told Mama how pleasant her
kitchen seemed to a traveler, and how pretty she was looking. "I see the apples are back in your cheeks," he said. "Must
be these little ones are beginning to be good at last."

He reached over and patted the round yellow heads of
the twins. He winked at Sidney, telling him he'd had a look
at the beaver colony last spring after leaving their house.

"You got me so interested in them, I felt I had to see the
colony for myself. I took to the woods, you might say, after
I left here that morning. I followed the lake around to the
other side so I could study their houses near the shore. Mighty
interesting! I'd never seen anything like that before. Oh, I
know you're keeping it kind of quiet for fear someone would
get the idea of trapping. Don't worry—I haven't told anyone.
I just remembered it now as I came down the road again."

"You should see the shack Larry and I built on the island
last summer," put in Sidney eagerly. "We made a raft out of
logs and a barrel and poled across. We pretended we were
fur traders, holed up in the wilderness. As soon as the ice is
safe now, we're going over again and have a look around."

* 17 *

The peddler was peeling off layers of damp clothing, piling everything neatly on a chair beside the stove as Mama had told him to do. The kitchen had become a wonderfully pleasant place; Sidney and Elizabeth would not have gone out for anything now. When the peddler arrived so late in the day, he showed his wares in the evening and always stayed overnight.

"We were sure glad when we saw you coming," Sidney said as they sat down together beside the stove. Elizabeth was setting the table, and Mama was stirring up a batch of soda biscuits, the bread supply being low. "In weather like this, though, I bet you wish you had a horse and wagon like some peddlers, or a different job even. It must be tough walking on rainy days. You looked kinda tired as you came down the road. When I lived in Chicago—"

"Sure I was tired," said the peddler. "But I knew I'd soon be resting in this nice warm kitchen with fine folks like you. You have to keep thinking of such things when the going gets hard."

He tweaked Sidney's ears playfully, sensing what the frequent references to Chicago meant. The orphan was still living in the past, not quite happy in his new home. This had been very apparent to Yusef Hanna in the spring, and though he had just arrived, he could tell that the adjustment had not yet been made.

"Peddling's a pretty good life, you know—yes, even on foot," he continued. "When the roads are dry and the weather is even middling good, it can be very enjoyable."

The Coming of the Peddler

It seemed that "enjoy" must be one of the Laugh Peddler's favorite words, he used it so much. It was one not often spoken by the hard-working farmers of Lakeland Township. Nearly all of them had come as immigrants from North European countries. They were hard-working and occupied chiefly with their farms and their church, and they regarded the peddler's job with a certain disapproval. To them peddling was not a proper way of making a living. It did not seem suitable for a strong man to walk the roads while they worked in the fields, even though he did carry a heavy pack. The lightheartedness the peddler displayed made their sober natures uncomfortable.

But last spring Yusef Hanna had explained his job and his good nature to Sidney very sensibly: "It takes more than one kind of job to get the world's work done," he had said. "Now I would be a poor farmer no matter how I tried, seems like. I never learned the work—see? But I know peddling, and it makes a living. So why shouldn't I do the work I know and enjoy? And why not show that I enjoy it?"

When Sidney asked how he always remained cheerful, he answered carefully, as if he'd given the question serious thought, "The way I see it—a long face only lengthens your trouble. A laugh, why that puts it out of sight! A laugh is the lightest thing I carry, and it buys a lot of good will."

Now he was running a small comb through his black hair to bring order to the damp curling locks. Mama had sat down for a minute, and he chatted with her about the summer and the peddling business in general.

* 19 *

"Yup, it's been a pretty good season—though not quite as good as usual," he said. "I heard you had two hail storms in these parts just as the grain was ripening. That's made some difference in how people buy, naturally. Anyone knows what it does to a farmer's income when he loses his biggest crop. Too bad!"

Mama agreed sadly. "We lost both our barley stand and much of the wheat. But we still have our corn crop. And of course we depend on our cows—the milk checks—to see us through the winter."

The peddler clucked sympathetically. "Another year— another crop, eh? We all live for tomorrow, seems like. With me, it's the little notion store I'm going to have soon as I've saved a bit of money. I'm not saying I don't enjoy peddling, but a man's legs begin to give out in time. And with people buying autos more and more, they'll be driving to the city stores to do their buying."

His eyes were suddenly wistful. "And it is nice to stay home with one's family, too. My little Maggie was very sick in September. Bronchitis, the doctor said. She still coughs at night sometimes.

"But so!" He brightened. "One of these days I'll have my own little store, and the ladies will come to me to buy!"

Mama needed more wood for the stove, so Sidney hurried out to the woodshed and brought in an armful of stove lengths, piling them in the woodbox. Then he settled himself beside the peddler again.

He found this man indescribably cheering, and it had been

so ever since he had first seen him a few weeks after he had arrived in his new home, a bereft, bewildered boy. With both parents dead, he knew that he no longer had a home in Chicago, but still his thoughts kept returning stubbornly to that city. He remembered the bustle and the bright lights, the lighthearted cheer of the little flat on Halsted Street. Here in the country, he had found the early spring land-scape cold and bleak, and there was no one who seemed to understand him when he talked of the city's charm.

But the peddler, whose home was in St. Paul, understood, and he could bring the world of the big city close to Sidney again. They held companionable discussions about brightly lighted stores, noisy streetcars, clanging fire engines, and the gay, colorful bustle of city streets at holiday time. And then, too, the peddler's unfailing good cheer was something like that of his own lost father. He had a way of cheering you up, no matter how you felt.

It was Yusef Hanna who had succeeded in making Sidney laugh out loud on that gray day in early spring when he first met him. It was the first time he had laughed in months. Sid-ney was not sure just how the peddler did it; it wasn't any funniness you could really describe, but it was a way he had of teasing the laughter out of you. This was how he had earned the name "the Laugh Peddler." No one could say exactly how it had started, but there were many who did not even know his real name, the nickname fitted him so well.

Supper was on the table, and Mama called everyone to take their places. Papa and Karl had come in from the corn crib and barn, acknowledging the peddler's presence with the briefest of nods. They washed in silence. Everyone became a bit subdued, and supper was eaten swiftly, because there was still much work to be done outside before nightfall.

"Sure to turn to snow," said Papa darkly to Karl. "You didn't get started on the straw shelter for the young stock yet. We've got to have it up before cold weather strikes."

Karl looked troubled. "I'll get at it tomorrow morning. There's just too much work on this place for two men," he concluded.

Karl was a younger cousin of Papa's who had come from Germany two years before, and was working as his hired man until he got his American citizenship papers. He endured the hard work, long hours, and the low pay without complaint, because he felt it was worth any sacrifice to become an American citizen. Only now and then, when he felt overworked, he would show his resentment toward Sidney in little ways that Sidney found humiliating. Karl knew all too well that many twelve-year-old farm boys were almost as good as men when it came to everyday work.

Though unable to help with the milking, Sidney went out to the barn after supper with the men. When it was time to take care of the horses, he was allowed to feed them their oats and fill their mangers with hay. Sometimes while the milking was going on, he rubbed and curried them, a luxury farm work horses seldom knew. But Sidney knew and loved horses from Chicago, where he had often gone to the livery stable with his father when they were going for a Sunday drive and wanted to rent a rig. The stable attendants there had let him do things around the horses, so he had come to understand them.

After Sidney and the men went out, Elizabeth washed the supper dishes and Mama got the twins ready for bed, though they would be allowed to stay up for a while, this being a special evening.

When everything was done, Mama sat down in the rocker, holding both babies in her lap. Elizabeth, bright-eyed with eagerness, found chairs for herself and Sidney, who had hurried in as soon as he had fed the horses. They sat waiting for the opening of the pack.

Always there was something new, some beautiful thing they had never seen before—usually down at the bottom of the pack. Last spring it had been a little music box with a pearly cover, topped with a dancing fairy. When opened, it played tinkly music that almost made you see fairies dancing by moonlight. They knew that it had come from one of the big city stores—maybe even from Europe. Even though it could not be bought, just to see and touch something like that was a privilege. And with the Laugh Peddler talking and joking as he took pains to show everything, it was better than any show.

Since the peddler was to spend the night, he could take his time with the showing. Mama had explained to him that as usual she had no good place for him in the house, but he could sleep in the barn hayloft as he had done before. "I have plenty of blankets so you won't freeze even if the weather turns bad," she said, adding, "I can't understand what happened to my warmest, best quilt; it disappeared off the line yesterday. Anyway, I have plenty of others for you to take out."

The peddler agreed cheerfully to the sleeping arrangements. The hayloft was clean and spacious, and farm homes were always a bit cramped for room. Mrs. Miller was a fine cook, and their home was centrally located in a good selling area. He liked to make it his headquarters for the two or three days he worked these roads. Wherever he stayed, he gave as payment some merchandise out of his pack. This time it was to be a length of dress silk, chosen by his hostess for herself.

After all the arrangements had been made, Mrs. Miller added hastily that of course he would not smoke in the barn. She was sure he remembered how much Papa was against it because of the danger of fire.

"I smoke only on the road," the peddler answered easily. "A pipe is a bit of company when I walk, seems like. But when I go to bed I'm much too tired for anything but sleeping. Don't worry, dear lady."

2. The Pack Is Opened

Everything was ready at last, and the peddler turned to the business of opening the pack. He unbuckled each strap carefully and lifted the top. Then he began showing his wares, as if it were an important rite that must not be hurried.

On top were the linens—scarves and doilies and tablecloths. He lifted each piece, turning it deftly in his hands, explaining the quality of the goods, how it was made, and where it came from. It seemed to make no difference to him whether his things were bought or merely admired. The children were fascinated by all he knew.

"Pretty, eh?" he would say, or "Nice goods!" touching the fabric with careful hands.

Under the linens were the yard goods, and Mama now

bought a length of white cambric. She did not mention what it was for, but Elizabeth needed a petticoat, and this cloth seemed to fit the purpose. Below the yard goods were laces —some Syrian handmade and some from American machine looms. They were all lovely.

"This would go nicely with the cambric," he said, holding up a length of dainty lace. "It's strong though it looks delicate." He pulled it between his fingers to show its strength, then seeing the expression on Mama's face, he rolled it up again quickly. "A good seamstress can make a nice garment without lace, too," he added hastily.

It was quite clear from the expression on Elizabeth's face that she would like to have lace on her petticoat, however. Many of the girls in school did, and they managed to wear their dresses a trifle short so the lace showed when they walked, or flounced out prettily when they sat down.

Suddenly the peddler took out a big feather fan, unfolding it under her nose. "Hey, little owl," he said, tickling her nose with the feathers. "Let's see if the space between your front teeth has filled in since last spring."

She laughed out suddenly and wriggled out of his reach. Everyone was laughing except the peddler; he was now very serious.

"That laugh costs you twenty-five cents," he said. "It was a small one, but I have them in bigger sizes, too. They cost up to a dollar and come in many different colors."

There was an uproarious laugh at this. Laughs in color— how ridiculous! And did the peddler really think he could

sell laughs—for money? Only *things* cost money! No one, except the Laugh Peddler, ever mentioned money and laughter in the same breath.

Last spring after he had left, Elizabeth and Sidney had talked about it. Why was the peddler so different from Papa and other men around there? Sidney said wistfully that in some ways he reminded him of his father, who had always tried to make light of everything, including his illness.

Elizabeth wondered if it was because he came from such a different country. No one that they knew had come from a place that was warm all the year around. He described his native Syria as "a sunny little paradise." But why then had he left it? They meant to ask him some day.

Finally Sidney had concluded thoughtfully, "I guess he thinks that there are a lot of things that make you happy and they don't cost any money either. Cheerfulness is one of them. Sometimes you'd really think it cost money to laugh around here!"

Below the laces were a few lengths of dress silk, and Mama now had the privilege of choosing one of them as her payment for keeping the peddler during his stay. She could not decide between a plain dark blue and a creamy yellow with lavender stripes. Holding them both up to the lamp, she studied the texture of the material. Finally, with the help of everyone in the room, including Papa and Karl, who had come in from the barn, she chose the yellow and lavender. It seemed to set off her brown hair and soft, rosy coloring the best.

The Pack Is Opened

"That piece of goods should be yours, Mrs. Miller," said the Laugh Peddler gallantly. "You compliment the colors, seems like."

Mama was pleased and practical, too. "It will go both with my summer hat and with the lace collar from my old dress. All I'll have to buy is hooks and thread and such things. It's a good piece of silk. I have the feeling I'm getting the best of the bargain."

The Laugh Peddler patted his stomach and smiled. "I'm getting a bargain in meals," he said. "Maybe I'll be sitting down to one of your pancakes and sorghum and sausage breakfasts tomorrow, eh?"

Mama knew that she had a reputation for making the best pork sausage in the neighborhood, and they had butchered just last week. The crocks were full of freshly made sausages and meatballs, seasoned her own special way.

The peddler had shown nearly everything in his pack now. He rummaged around at the bottom where he kept the buttons, the packets of hairpins, the buckles, and other trinkets. Mama bought what she needed of these. Elizabeth had detected a white box as he stirred around among the articles.

"Another music box?" she asked. "Won't you please let us see it?"

"No music box; something else quite special," said the peddler.

He picked up the box, opened it, and unwrapped the tissue paper inside to reveal a pair of yellow tortoise-shell combs that sparkled as if set with diamonds. There were gasps of admiration. These were simply the most beautiful side-combs anyone had ever seen.

"They would go nicely with your dress silk," said the peddler. He held them up and turned them slowly so the light caught on the dazzling rhinestones. "Combs matching the dress are a Paris fashion."

Mama reached up hastily to smooth her hair, trying to tuck in the little escaping locks that hung down over neck and ears. "How much?" she asked softly.

"Four-fifty. See, it's genuine tortoise shell, not imitation. And these are real Austrian rhinestones." He looked almost apologetic. After a moment he added, "For you, I make it four."

Mama sighed and her eyes sought her husband's, but he was staring intently at the ceiling. Sidney studied the patches on his overalls. The twins held out their hands to catch the flashes of light thrown out by the glittering rhinestones. Elizabeth sat staring at the combs as if unable to take her eyes away from them.

But even Sidney knew that four dollars for a fancy pair of combs was out of the question here. The fine big calf Papa had sold last week had not brought that much—after weeks of care and feeding. And the milk checks were getting lower as they always did in winter months. You could hardly blame farmers for getting discouraged and downhearted, he decided.

Just last Saturday, when he and Elizabeth were with Papa to get shoes at the Company Store, he had pointed to a

Flexible Flyer sled, saying, "That's the kind of sled Daddy promised me for my birthday. It's the best kind there is. If he'd lived, I'd have had one."

Papa, overhearing, spoke a bit grimly. "When you're on a farm you have to learn to get along with second best. And sometimes you don't even get that!"

Mama broke the awkward silence. "Well, I'll have to get the silk made up first, and that may not be until spring. Things are so busy now just before Christmas that I couldn't get sewing help for weeks anyway. So I really wouldn't have any use for the combs now."

But she spoke unconvincingly. Anyone could tell she would be very glad to have them now. They might easily be sold by spring.

It was apparent that the Laugh Peddler thought so, too. He explained that they were the last rhinestone combs he had. They were imported from Austria, and with the war getting worse over there, he was not likely to have any more for a long time. He wrapped them in tissue paper again and put them back in their box, wedging it into a space at the bottom of the pack.

"Well, that's the lot," he said, beginning to repack the portmanteau. "The load will be a bit lighter tomorrow, and by week's end when I return to St. Paul, it will hardly be any load at all."

Suddenly he turned in his chair so the table lamp was behind him. He put his hands together, crooking some fingers and twisting or straightening others.

"Now a little show for the babies," he said. "They've been so good, though they're getting tired. Watch the wall now—don't look at me." They turned their eyes obediently.

"We're going to have a circus right here in the kitchen," said the peddler. Sure enough, the shadow of a large rooster appeared on the wall, flapped its wings, stretched its neck and opened its beak. There was a sudden sharp crow, so natural and unexpected that even Papa laughed in surprise.

Once before, the Laugh Peddler had made shadow pictures in this kitchen, but neither Sidney nor the twins had seen them then. They sat quiet, waiting for whatever would come next. Obviously, the peddler had not shown quite everything yet. He turned to Sidney who had laughed loudest at the rooster. "I charge you fifty cents for that laugh," he said. "It carries a double guarantee. Money back if not satisfied."

Once more he told them to look at the wall. Suddenly an elephant lumbered across it, and only Sidney, who had moved close, knew that a cleverly twisted scarf helped to produce the illusion. Then a monkey hung from a branch, chattering shrilly, and a turtle came creeping along. After, came a hopping rabbit, long ears and all. And with the shadow pictures were sound effects or story lines.

Now and then as the laughter welled up, the peddler would stop and make an imaginary sale, shaking his head with pretended seriousness. At last he said, "No, now I have to stop. I'm almost sold out, and I'll go out of business if I extend any more credit."

The Pack Is Opened

"Play for us, or sing a song, then—the way you did last spring," begged Sidney. He couldn't bear for the evening to end.

Yusef Hanna took a harmonica from his pocket and played in rollicking rhythm a jolly tune that immediately had Sidney and Elizabeth clapping their hands in accompaniment. Then he put the instrument aside and began singing. It was a Syrian song with words they did not understand, but his pleasant baritone made it sound beautiful. When he finished his eyes were thoughtful, and Mama asked him what it was about.

"It's a story about my home city—Edessa, in Syria," he explained. "It's a very old city—said to be one of the very first Christian cities—and in the time of our Lord it was ruled by a good king named Abgar Ukama. I have seen the ancient document in the city archives that tells how King Abgar, having heard of Jesus Christ and his miracles, sent a message to Him asking Him to come to Edessa and heal him of an ailment he had. He wrote to Christ: 'I have heard that the leaders murmur against you and seek to harm you. The city I have is small and stately; there is room in it for us both.'

"And the story goes that Jesus sent his blessing in reply, though he was unable to travel so far. A church historian tells the same story; Eusebius is his name. You may have read it in his church history."

Mama murmured her appreciation, and even Papa, who taught Sunday school, was impressed. He cleared his throat to say, "Church history has many interesting stories, but I never heard of that one, though I've heard of Eusebius, of course."

Elizabeth studied the Laugh Peddler with interest. "If you come from such a good city, why did you want to leave? You must have had a lot of good things in such a nice place."

Yusef Hanna laughed. "Oh my, no! I had nothing! My father died when I was very small and my mother scratched out a living for the two of us until I was old enough to work myself. I worked in fruit markets—wherever they needed and would take someone like me. I did the jobs no one else would do—and lived mostly on sunshine and fruit!"

"But if it was so warm and nice—and your mother was there?" pursued Elizabeth.

"Well, when I was sixteen, my Uncle Yusef—my mother's brother, see—wrote saying the living was better in America. He was working out of St. Paul as a peddler and said it was good work and I could do it. I could learn from him. He sent passage money, but before we could take ship, my mother suddenly became ill and died. And so I came alone. That's how it was in Syria—sunshine and history, but no good way to make a living for those born poor.

"But how about you singing a song now, Mrs. Miller? I heard you once when you were rocking the babies there; you have a lovely voice. You sang a Swedish song; as I remember it was a spinning song. With such a voice you should sing more often."

The Pack Is Opened

Mama blushed with pleasure. As a young girl in Sweden she had loved to sing and had often heard her voice praised for its sweetness. But here in Minnesota it seemed that there was little time for singing, except when a child was in need of soothing.

She began a little timidly at first; then, her sweet voice increasing in strength, she sang the plaintive song about a young girl who sat spinning while waiting for her true love to return from across the ocean:

> *"Spinn, spinn, dotter minn;*
> *Snart sa kommer friarn dinn...."*

> ("Spin, spin, daughter mine;
> Soon will come your sweetheart....")

The mother of the spinning maiden sought to comfort her with these words, but the true love never returned, being lost at sea or something.

Mama was not quite sure about the words of the last stanza, so she never sang the saddest part. Little Ernest found being sung to by his mother such a treat that he lay back in her arms and fell fast asleep.

The spirit of musical entertainment caught Papa, too. He began to sing an old German song remembered from childhood. Ellen, on his knee, recognized it as the "rocking-horse song" and quickly slid down his long leg. She set herself astride his big foot as he began kicking in time to the music.

The tune had a military rocking rhythm, which was matched by the words:

*"Da reiten die Herren/Mit blanken Gewehren,
Sie reiten auf Fohlen/Mit blanken pistolen—Hussah!"*

("There ride the gentlemen/With glittering big guns,
They ride the young steeds/With glittering pistols—
Hurrah!")

Ellen screamed with delight as Papa kicked his leg higher and higher. Ernest awoke, and sliding off Mama's lap, ran to Papa, begging "Wanna reiten die herren too!" They began slapping each other with small angry hands when Ellen refused to get off her "horse." Ernest's screams of indignation grew loud.

Mama rose quickly. "That's enough! Bedtime for both of you; it's an hour late already. Fred, I know that's supposed to be a jolly song, but I just don't care for it. It makes soldiering and war seem fine and glorious. For the children's sake I wish you wouldn't sing it any more. With the terrible war going on over there, and some of your own relatives in it, it is—it reminds—" She stopped suddenly, shivering.

"That's how it was over there, though," said Karl quietly from the woodbox corner. "You could see it in everything. In Prussia where my home was, even the children mostly played war games. I saw it often. That is why I wanted to get away from there so much." He stopped, looking faintly embarrassed.

The Pack Is Opened

Everyone was silent, and all the early good cheer seemed gone. Papa looked worried again as he began to bank the fire in the stove.

"Hurry, children," said Mama briskly, wrapping each twin in a small woolly blanket that had been warming behind the stove. "Put the babies in bed right away and don't linger over undressing, but get in bed quickly and don't lie awake talking. Remember what a long walk you have to school in the morning."

Sidney and Elizabeth began climbing the stairs, each holding a twin by the hand. They looked back, calling good night to the peddler, who began strapping up his portmanteau in preparation for his next day of selling.

Mama was busy in the pantry getting things in order for the morning's early breakfast, and Papa whittled kindling for the fires. Karl had already disappeared to his cold room over the parlor.

The long delightful evening was over. But there would be others, as long as Yusef Hanna was there. You couldn't exactly describe it, but there was something almost magical in the way he brightened everything for a while—something even better than the things he carried in his pack, nice as they were.

3. Sidney Thinks of a Way

In spite of Mama's admonitions, Sidney and Elizabeth lay talking after they were in bed. The door separating their rooms stood open, and it was hard to keep silent in the darkness. Elizabeth snuggled close to Ellen's balled-up little frame to get warm. Their bedroom, over the kitchen, was a bit warmer than Sidney's and Ernest's over the chilly dining room. Even so, it was always hard to get warm after undressing in the upstairs cold.

Elizabeth called softly to Sidney, "Are you awake? I'm not at all sleepy, are you?"

His answer came with a shiver. "I'm not even warm yet. My feet are like ice. The bed is so cold!"

Elizabeth sighed and yawned. "You'll get warm; I already am. But, oh, I wish we could think of a way Mama could have those combs! Weren't they beautiful? They'd make a perfect Christmas present—even better than Larry's old locket and chain from the big store in Minneapolis!"

Sidney put his back against Ernest's and spoke toward the open door. "I think I know a way," he said. "I'll tell it to you in the morning."

"Tell me now," coaxed Elizabeth. "I want to know before I go to sleep."

"Well, see—it's the way Daddy and Mummy bought things sometimes when we lived in Chicago. If they had some money but not enough, they went to the store and paid what they could on the thing. That's called a 'down payment.' Then afterwards they paid some money every month—an 'installment' they called it. That way we got the thing we wanted right away, and we could pay for it a little at a time as we got more money."

"Would it be like going in debt?" asked Elizabeth anxiously. "'Cause Papa and Mama don't like that. They won't even charge things at the Company Store like Larry's folks do."

"No, it's not exactly like a debt," said Sidney. "Debts last a long time, and sometimes they never get paid off. But this way—well, say we put what money we have together—it makes seventy-five cents—and give it to the Laugh Peddler as our 'down payment.' And we promise to send the rest when we get it, in one or two 'installments.' He wouldn't have to wait very long. I may get to earn some money on Christmas vacation. Larry said his father will be fanning his grain then—they have a lot of it you know—and Larry said he'd ask if I could help, and then I'd get paid. That way I might even earn a couple of dollars."

"And I'm sure to get some from Aunt Huldah for Christmas," broke in Elizabeth. "She always sends some money with the thing she knits or crochets for me. Last year it was my red fascinator scarf—there was a little pocket knitted into it, and in it there was a whole dollar!"

"Well, there's three dollars right there!" said Sidney. "You see that's why it wouldn't really be a debt. We'd be able to make the payments on time; we might even pay it all off in about a month. I'll talk to the Laugh—"

Mama's firm step could be heard on the stairs. There was no opportunity for further planning now. The children closed their eyes and went quickly to sleep.

When Sidney was sent to the barn to call the peddler for breakfast, he told him first that the pancakes and sausage were ready. "There's just about everything anyone could want for breakfast today—even chokecherry syrup for the pancakes. I never tasted that before I came here, and now it's my favorite. She's an awfully good cook."

"Don't I know it?" said Yusef Hanna, standing up with alacrity. "There's no one can beat a good Swedish cook— unless it's a Syrian girl maybe." He put on his coat and followed Sidney out through the wide hayloft door.

The rain had stopped during the night and it had turned colder. An ominous grayness hung over the landscape, sug-

gesting that fall weather had ended and that winter was
beginning.

"Smells like snow is on the way," said the peddler, sniffing the air. "I do hope it doesn't come before I've finished
my selling. I'd planned on two, three more days at least,
before I lay up for the winter."

Sidney spoke of the thing uppermost in his mind as they
walked to the house. "Say," he began, "Elizabeth and I
like those rhinestone combs very much, and we'd like to
buy them for a Christmas present for Mama. Do you suppose you could—well, kind of hold them out and not sell
them to anyone else? We have part of the money to make
a down payment with. You know about those, don't you?
And I'm sure to earn some money during Christmas vacation, so we could—we think we'd be able to pay the rest..."
He looked anxiously into the peddler's face.

"Why, sure," came the cheerful answer, as if this were
the most common arrangement in the world to a peddler.
"I'll keep them for you, since you've spoken for them.
That's a promise. When I finish my selling at week's end,
we'll complete the transaction; I'll take the down payment
and you get the combs."

Sidney told Elizabeth how well his plan had worked as
they walked to school. "It's all fixed," he said. "I talked
to the Laugh Peddler this morning, and he understands
about down payments and installment buying. He'll let us
have the combs with the money we have."

Elizabeth's admiration for Sidney's cleverness gave him

great pleasure. She spoke almost humbly of how little she knew of business transactions like this. "If we manage to get Mama the best Christmas present she's ever had, it will be because you're so smart," she said.

The school day passed swiftly, much of the time being taken up with preparations for the Christmas program. A few large snowflakes began to fall at noon, and by the time the children walked home in the afternoon, there was a thin carpet of white over the rutted, frozen road. Larry whooped with joy, for it meant that there would soon be enough snow for skiing, and he was already able to ski the long hill in their pasture. Both the boys looked forward to roaming wherever they pleased on their skis—especially over to the island. Last winter Sidney had used an old pair of Pa's, a bit large, but he had got used to them and managed to keep up with the more expert Larry.

"Pa said this morning the ice is thick on the lake now. In fact, it's been safe two or three days, but he wouldn't tell me before." Larry turned in at his own road, adding, "Pa and Ma can't forget about that kid who broke through a couple of years ago, even though that was early November, when anyone knows lake ice isn't safe. I guess he knows we want to make for the island."

"Maybe we could go over this afternoon?" Sidney called. "I don't have anything to do except my usual chores."

"I can't today. I have to go to my uncle's," Larry called back. "They're butchering, and we have to help. We go tomorrow, too. But maybe Saturday I can go with you."

Sidney Thinks of a Way

Elizabeth was pleased when Sidney turned to her, asking her to accompany him, though she knew she was only a substitute for Larry on any adventuring trip.

"Do you think your Papa will let us?" asked Sidney. "I left my jackknife over there in the shack last summer. It's the one I got from Daddy, and I want to get it before it's all rusted."

"I'm sure Papa won't mind as long as it's safe. Especially if you tell him that we want to see how the beavers are getting along. He's so proud of that beaver colony! Just tell him we want to go over and look at the beavers, and he'll say it's all right."

It was, however, with some trepidation that Sidney went to the woodshed and confronted Papa with his request. "We want to see if the beavers are getting along all right," he concluded hopefully.

Papa, chopping wood for the stoves, seemed interested. "Lucky we got that beaver-protection law through a couple of years ago," he said. "If we hadn't, there would be no colony over there to see, you can be sure. They'd be killed off here in this state as they have been to the east. I'm real proud of helping get that law passed. Larsen and I wrote almost a dozen letters to the Legislature, between the two of us."

"Larry and I saw them working on their houses last summer," Sidney went on. "We even watched a couple of them chewing off a little tree for their dam in the creek on the other side of the lake."

Sidney Thinks of a Way

"That so?" Papa stopped work to wipe the sweat off his face. "That's a thing I've never even seen myself. Goes on in summer, and that's such a busy time here."

Sidney suddenly felt emboldened enough to confide the secret uppermost in his and Elizabeth's mind. "You know we—Elizabeth and I—are going to buy those combs from the peddler and give them to Mama for Christmas. I talked to him this morning. He's going to let us pay what money we have—seventy-five cents—on account, and then we'll pay the rest later when we get it."

Papa looked pleased. "Well, that should make Mama real happy," he said. "I couldn't see my way to buy them with times so hard, but in a month or so I can help you—if you haven't got the rest of the money by then. And I'll tell you what I'll do now. If you could help us with the young stock shelter now, maybe you can go to the island tomorrow. Then if it snows enough, you can take the big milk sled and haul back a load of wood. I'll pay you twenty-five cents for that wood, so you can make a dollar your first payment. Our wood supply is low, and the sawyers don't come until next week. There's plenty of dead wood lying around there; it's state land and so it's not picked up like here. But as long as it's on the ground, we can take it. Do you think you could manage to do all that?"

Sidney was jubilant over the responsibilities offered him, and cheered by the way Papa had talked to him. It was man-to-man, as it used to be with Daddy. It must mean that Papa was beginning to like him a little better.

"Oh, gee, thanks—Pa!" He added the last word softly.
He began to run off when he remembered something. "But
if you can't cut wood on the island, then who cut down
the big pine in the very middle of the island? It was cut
down before last summer, 'cause Larry and I built our shack
around the stump. It was so big and flat we called it our
table, and we used to pull our apple boxes up to it and eat
our lunches off it."

Papa's face showed his puzzlement. "I don't understand
why anyone would cut a tree there—with so much un-
cleared land on every farm. They surely didn't need it for
wood. Maybe—but no, it couldn't be—not after all these
years!"

He stood staring off into the distance as if seeing something altogether hidden from Sidney. "I'll tell you a story
about that island some time—maybe even tonight, if we get
through the chores early. It's a kind of mystery story you
might say, and I think you'll find it interesting. Now hurry
up and help us with that shelter. We must have it done
before dark. Maybe you can haul up the log braces on the
wheelbarrow; that isn't such a hard job. Take just three or
four at a time and they won't be too heavy."

Sidney ran to the barn to get the wheelbarrow. He was
in high spirits and could not resist making a running dive
into the hay. It still smelled almost as sweet as it had last
summer when it had just come in from the mow. He landed
near the hollowed-out place where the Laugh Peddler had
slept. It would be pleasant to sleep out here, thought Sid-

ney. No wonder Yusef Hanna called sleeping in the barn "my country vacation."

A hen flew out from the far corner of the loft and began cackling loudly. Sidney had been on the farm long enough to understand what that meant. She was laying her eggs in a place where Mama could not find them, no doubt planning to hatch herself a brood of chickens, though it was the wrong time of year for such ventures. If the eggs were fresh, he'd fool Mrs. Hen and bring them into the house. He found the nest in the far corner of the loft near the horse stable, but there was only one egg in it and it was still warm.

"That's funny," he said to himself. "The nest certainly looks as if she'd been setting for quite a while."

He was about to pick up the egg and start back, when he saw another hollow in the hay, close to the hen's nest. It was lined with a gray horse blanket and beside it lay Mama's lost quilt and a sheepskin coat that looked like Karl's.

"So that's where Doogan dragged the quilt," thought Sidney, but then immediately realized that old Doogan could not have been responsible. Even a big sheep dog was not strong enough to drag both a quilt and a heavy horse blanket into the hay. And besides, Doogan slept in the horse barn nights—in Tom's manger. It was a puzzle Sidney could not solve—at the moment anyway. He started toward the house with the quilt and met Papa on the way.

"Haven't you got the wheelbarrow yet? Hurry with

those poles; I told you we had to get through before dark."
Papa was impatient with him again, giving him no time to
explain.

There was time only to run to the house and hand the
quilt to Mama with a word of explanation about where it
had been. For the next hour Sidney worked hard, helping
to get the stock shelter finished. His arms ached from pushing the wheelbarrow back and forth almost on the run,
but he kept up. Papa had no cause to speak to him harshly
again.

4. Papa Tells a Story

When the stock shelter was finished, it was strong and snug enough to withstand even the hard winter storms. The tired men trooped into the house, Sidney following. He felt almost a part of the family now; he had done his share of an important piece of work. He did not mind the exhaustion, though he was too tired to do his arithmetic. With luck he could manage to do it tomorrow while the younger classes were up reciting.

The family was just sitting down to supper when the peddler plodded in wearily. He had walked farther than usual in his eagerness to cover the territory before bad weather put an end to his year's selling.

"Oh, how good to get back!" he sighed, unstrapping his

pack. "But a big day I had! Everyone wants to buy some extras for Christmas if possible. I walked and walked and showed and showed! I must have opened and closed my portmanteau at least two dozen times. Now if bad weather holds off just one more day I'll be ready to go back at week's end, and very thankful for a good season too."

"Did you sell all your laughs?" asked Elizabeth mischievously, as he sat down beside her at the table.

"All but one—a good big one I'm saving just for you." He winked slyly at Sidney and pinched her cheek. Both children understood that he was referring to their private secret—the purchase of the combs. Nothing could make them happier than this achievement.

After supper Papa consulted the *Farmers' Almanac* and noted that a storm was due soon. This made it necessary to get the young stock from the lower pasture into the shelter as soon as possible. "I'd thought we could wait till morning, but if bad weather's coming we'd best get them in now."

As they lighted the lanterns, Sidney suddenly remembered the other sleeping place in the hayloft. "Say," he began, "I saw something funny up in the hayloft this afternoon—where I found the quilt. Doogan never dragged it up there; he couldn't. It was way over in the far corner. It looked as if somebody—"

Karl opened the door hastily. "Beginning to snow again," he said. "If I'm going to get those steers in, I'll need help. Even you might do. They're going to be wild after being out so long. Come on—get your coat on. Hurry!"

"That's right," said Papa, swallowing the last of his coffee and getting up hastily. "No time to lose—darkness coming on and no moon. And we must take care of the steers; they're like money in the bank."

When the stock was safely in the shelter and the horses fed, Sidney's arms and legs ached with weariness. He returned slowly to the house, hoping for time to talk a little with the Laugh Peddler before bed time. But Yusef Hanna was worn out, too, and had already gone to his hayloft bed. Elizabeth sat on her chair near the stove, and Mama was making fruit soup for tomorrow's breakfast. The twins had been put to bed.

But when Papa came in, Sidney, tired though he was, reminded him of his promise to tell the story of the island. For months now he and Larry had quite properly felt that it was their island since they had built the shack on it and were its only inhabitants. If there was a story about it, Sidney felt they should know it. That way their trips over there—when they pretended to be hunters or fur traders or Indians—would be even more exciting.

Papa had settled down at the table with a grain sack that needed mending. He too would be fanning grain soon, though his crop was small this year and the whole process would take only about a day.

He was holding the large needle close to the lamp, squinting as he tried to thread it. When this was done and the knot in, he laid the patch in place carefully and began to sew.

"Oh, yes, the story," he said. "But you ought to be in

bed, you know. It's close to nine." Seeing Sidney's look of disappointment, he said, "Oh, well, it won't take long to tell it. I guess you can stay up a little while."

He took a few careful stitches, then laid the sack down. "Well, to start with," he began, "I want you to know that I don't put much stock in that story myself. It's one of those tales I heard from old Erik years ago. He's the settler who homesteaded the Larsen place and lived there until he died and they bought it. Seems he'd known a bachelor fellow, name of Arne Nord, back there in the sixties, the time of the Civil War, who'd been a hunter and had trapped and traded with the Indians quite a lot. He'd made a nice little pile of money for himself, mostly on furs; beaver I suppose. His brother was old Jonas Nord who lived on the place he homesteaded, on the other side of Big Lake. His son, John Nord, lives there now, the one who had the corn-binder accident this fall. Well, that was where Arne lived, the fellow this story is about.

"Right off when the Civil War started, Arne was against the Confederacy. It wasn't so much the Abolition cause as that he'd had some trouble down there when he worked in a mill in a southern state a while before. He'd lost money in a bank down there too. So he had a grudge against the South and soon after war was declared, he up and enlisted in the Union Army. His only worry was what to do with his money since he didn't put faith in banks any more.

"Old Erik was about the only friend Arne had I guess. Of course, he wasn't old then; he was in his thirties some-

where, like Arne. As boys they'd hunted and fished together and gone over to the island, about the way you and
Larry do now. But Arne was close-mouthed, though, and
never told Erik what he planned to do.

"Only on the day before he left for the War, he came
over there and asked to use Erik's boat—said he wanted to
row over to the island again. All Erik knew was he brought
a spade and a box with him—looked like a little strong box.
But he asked no questions and Arne gave no information.
He must have been an odd, suspicious kind of fellow. He
came back without the box, said good-by and drove off and
that was the last Erik ever saw of him. He was wounded
toward the end of the war, and died in a southern prison
hospital."

Sidney's eyes were wide. "D'you think he buried the box
on the island? It must have been a money box, don't you
think? Then that would make it Treasure Island—just like
in the book I'm reading! But didn't anyone ever go over
there and dig it up? I mean—he must have told someone in
his own family where he hid the money."

"Who knows?" Papa folded the mended sack carefully
and stood up. "His brother Jonas must have known, but he
got secretive, too, it seems. Erik saw him go over to the
island a couple of times. He borrowed the boat, too, like
others did now and then, only he took along some digging
tools. But if he found anything, he never let on.

"Erik asked him once if he was digging for treasure, and
he answered him, kind of mean-like, 'Somebody got ahead

of me.' Seemed almost as if he suspected Erik of stealing the money. They were never real friendly after that.

"And the woods were full of beaver trappers and hunters, so he had no business suspecting Erik of stealing. Most likely—if there was a money box and if it was stolen—it was one of them found it. There always were beaver at that end of the lake and those years the market was wide open. And some years you can wade the narrow channel between the mainland and the island. But—well, Erik was a great one for stories, and I found out not all of them were true, either. He might just have imagined there was a money box—or for that matter, made up the whole thing."

"But why the digging then?" interposed Sidney. "Jonas wouldn't have taken digging tools over there just for the fun of it."

"That's so," agreed Papa. "That does make it seem as if there might be some truth in the story. With old Jonas still around, Erik wouldn't likely have made up that part; anyone could have gone over and asked him. He was a grumpy old coot, but he'd have told you soon enough if Erik was lying about the whole thing. I never heard that anyone came right out and asked him, though; he kept to himself so much. I'd have forgotten the whole thing, but today when you spoke of the chopped-down pine tree, I couldn't help wondering if there's some connection. One of these days' I'll go over myself and have a look."

Mama broke the silence briskly. "I heard that story years ago—when I was a newcomer from Sweden. I'd quite forgotten it too. Anyway it's after nine now, so to bed with you! If you'd known old Erik as we did, you wouldn't put much stock in the story. He was a terrible old windbag in his later years."

Elizabeth hurried up the stairs to bed, but Sidney got up from his chair as if in a dream. He climbed the stairs slowly and undressed in the cold room. He did not believe the story was a fabrication. The whole thing made sense to him as he marshalled the facts: the trip to the island by Arne Nord, and afterwards by his brother, the cut-down pine tree, even the grumpy old man, Jonas Nord, believing a neighbor had stolen a money box that should rightfully be his. Those things were not half so strange or unbelievable as the story he was reading about an old map hidden in a dead man's sea chest, a parrot screaming "pieces of eight!" from the shoulder of smooth-talking rogue with a "timber leg," while a boy his own age lay hidden in an apple barrel in a ship's galley, overhearing the plotting of a gang of pirates. Compared with *Treasure Island* this was a reasonable story.

"Just suppose," he said to himself, "just suppose I had a bit of money and was going away for quite a while, and I had lost money in banks so I didn't put any faith in them. What would I do with it?"

What better place to stash it than over on that lonely, wild island? And if Arne Nord had been on the island enough to observe its isolation, wouldn't the same idea naturally occur to him?

THE LAUGH PEDDLER

When he finally slept, Sidney dreamed of running from a pirate's nest in the shack, with Long John pursuing him as he fled across the frozen lake.

5. The Barn Is On Fire!

He was awakened by Mama's hand clutching at the bed-clothes. She stood over him, white-faced and shivering. The glass chimney on the lamp she held wobbled dangerously in her shaking hands.

"The barn is on fire! Hurry, Sidney, get up! You must help. The cows and horses are all in there. It's burning close to the stable already, the way it looks. Hurry!" She pulled off the heavy quilts to get him fully awake.

Sidney shook off his dream and leaped out of bed. He reached for his overalls and found them at once. Elizabeth was awakened too and came out of her room sleepily.

Mama, already on her way downstairs, called back again: "Hurry, both of you! You can help with the wet towels,

Elizabeth. Three of the neighbors are here already. We must pump up water from the cistern to soak towels for them to wrap around their faces; then they don't breathe in smoke as they fight the fire. They'll try to keep it from spreading until the fire department can get here from Foreston."

Sidney was downstairs almost on Mama's heels, while Elizabeth was still struggling with the problem of finding her clothes. Mama explained that the fire appeared to have started in the hayloft. The black smoke billowed thickly where the big double doors stood open. Here and there under the smoke an angry tongue of flame licked out.

Mama peered out of the kitchen windows. She seemed about to cry and plucked nervously at her shawl. "It may already be too late," she said. "When a barn begins burning this way at night, the fire gets too much of a start and the whole thing burns to the ground."

Sidney could feel her trembling as she helped him into his coat and handed him the pail of damp towels. He tried to think of something hopeful to say to reassure her, but again the situation was so new he could think of little in the way of comfort. He was doubtful and scared himself.

"You know the fire department saved Larsen's house a couple of years ago, and nobody thought they'd be able to do that, Larry said. He says they're the best fire fighters this side of St. Paul, even if they still use horses, and most towns already use motorized outfits. Larry says those horses are really fast!"

As he ran down the porch steps with the pail, old Doogan

leaped out of the shadows, whining. He was plainly frightened by the fire and had tried to get as close to the house as
possible.

Sidney thought of the horses then. The heaviest smoke
seemed to be right next to the horse stable. He remembered
stories of horses driven out of burning barns, only to run
back to their stalls and be burned to death. He'd heard that
such things happened because to a horse the stall means
security; in a frightening situation he will go through anything, even flames, to get back to that security.

Would they be able to get Tom and Fanny out? The new
colt, born last spring, had been sold a few weeks ago. It had
been a real sorrow to Sidney at the time, for having helped
care for it, he had come to regard it as his pet. Now he was
glad little Prince was gone.

The new snow was trampled to sooty slush around the
barn doors. Sidney had not stopped for rubbers and his feet
were wet. He made out Papa's tall figure in the murky half-
light and ran to him, setting down the pail. "Mama said to
wrap these around your faces," he said. "She's soaking some
more. Is there something I should do?"

Papa scarcely seemed to notice him. The other men were
inside the upper level, fighting the fire with wet sacks,
shovels, rakes, and even an old flail. Their blackened faces
showed fright and a desperate kind of fury. It appeared to
Sidney that they hardly expected to defeat the fire, but
they would go on fighting it angrily to the last.

A sudden lump came into his throat at the thought of all

this brave struggle wasted if the barn still burned down. It was like so many things a farmer did—sowing grain and tending it, only to have it taken when nearly ripe by hail, or raising cattle to have them die perversely of accidents or sudden diseases. It was an unfair battle.

Sidney grabbed a shovel and began to beat at a smoking mound of hay. He worked beside Mr. Larsen who was attacking it with the sack-wrapped flail.

A dull red glow was beginning to light a patch of clean snow outside the opposite door. It seemed already too late to put out the fire on that side. But the men fought on, trying to keep it in check. Everyone knew what it meant to a farmer to lose his barn. It was almost the worst disaster that could overtake him, especially with winter coming.

On the lower level, Karl was driving the cows out. He pricked them viciously with a pitchfork to hurry them, and they ran bawling in terror through the barnyard and out toward the newly erected shelter in the pasture. The calves followed, bellowing pitifully. It was a scene of wild confusion, but at least Karl was getting them out. The fire would in time burn through the hayloft floor and cave it in over anything left on the lower floor.

Some of the men were fighting the fire with water from the stock tank. They would drop their beating-out tools intermittently and run to pick up the buckets of water dipped out by Yusef Hanna at the pump. The peddler's eyes were no longer merry; they were anxious, and his movements showed a desperate eagerness to help.

The Barn Is On Fire!

Suddenly Papa called urgently to Sidney. "Get Tom and Fanny out! The stable may catch from a spark any time. The horses know you—put their bridles on and lead them out. Take them over to the yard fence and tie them up tight. Hurry!"

Sidney ran to the stable door and groped his way inside. He could tell at once that the horses were frightened by the smoke and the crackling noises just beyond the partition. They were stamping around in their stalls and giving short neighing screams of terror which sounded almost human. Sidney knew that he must get both of them out at once. The way it looked, there wouldn't be time for two trips.

He felt around in the smoky darkness until he found the bridles and halters on nails in the wall. It did not take him long to bridle the horses and snap on the halters. But it was another thing to lead them out. Fanny came willingly enough, but Tom hung back, rearing wildly at each step. Almost at once he broke away from Sidney's grasp and plunged back into the stall. Sidney groped his way back, still holding on to Fanny. Once again he took hold of Tom's halter, and by jerking and pulling succeeded in getting him to the door. But once there the horses refused to go forward. Fanny waited for Tom who was the lead horse, and Tom had begun rearing wildly. It took all Sidney's strength just to hold on to him.

The smoke was thickening to a cindery blackness now, but even in the murk Sidney could see how Tom's ears stood back and how his eyes rolled in terror. He bared his

teeth and flung up his head as if in agony. His flanks quivered as he braced his powerful legs to stay where he was.

Sidney's hands were blistering from the rope burns, and his eyes were smarting painfully. "Git! Giddap! Go, Tom boy!" Sidney panted in angry sobs. Tom, usually obedient to such words, now paid no attention. He continued to balk and utter short screaming neighs of protest.

Suddenly Sidney heard Yusef Hanna's voice speaking into his ear. The words were lost in the general confusion, but in the half-light Sidney watched the peddler quickly remove his long scarf and wrap it around Tom's head like a blindfold, so that his eyes were covered. His strong hand took the halter from Sidney's blistered grasp. "You hang on to Fanny," he said. "I'll get Tom out."

Unable to see the terrifying smoke and flames, Tom became almost docile and could be led out. Sidney followed with Fanny, and in a few minutes they had led both horses out of the stable and into the grove.

"I never could have done it without you!" cried Sidney, blowing his nose and almost weeping with relief. "I didn't know what to do! I just couldn't handle him. If you hadn't come. . . ."

The peddler quickly secured the knots that tied the horses to the fence. "Karl came and took my place at the tank—right after I saw you run into the stable," he explained. "I figured you'd be needing some help. I know how horses can behave in a fire."

From where they stood they could see the flames begin

to eat through the partitions and into the stalls of the horse stable. It would go just as Papa had said.

"You were saved just in time," said Sidney, stroking the trembling flanks of the horses. "You stupid old Tom—you'd be dying in there right now if you'd had your way."

He found the nearness of the Laugh Peddler comforting and edged close to him. But for once Yusef Hanna did not seem cheerful. He stood silent and uncertain, staring at the scene around the barn as if wondering what to do next.

"Will they save it, do you think?" asked Sidney.

"If the firemen get here very soon," he answered shortly, glancing up the road, "there might be a chance."

"You look as worried as if it was your barn," said Sidney. Then, remembering, he cried, "Your pack! Was it in the barn?"

"No, my portmanteau is safe in the house," answered the peddler, busying himself with the knots to make sure the horses were secure.

"Was it you who gave the alarm?" asked Sidney. "Lucky you were sleeping out there!"

The peddler spoke with mounting anger. "Yes, I gave the alarm. But I did not start the fire! And he—Mr. Miller—thinks that I did. Never in my life have I smoked in a barn. I know better! But it was no use to tell him that; he didn't believe me—he would not even listen! He said some hard things to me; they'll be hard to forget." The dark eyes in the smoke-blackened face were somber.

Until now Sidney had not even thought of the cause of

the fire. But of course—it must have been started by someone! And Pa naturally thought.... But anyone who knew
the Laugh Peddler would know that he never lied. He never
described his goods falsely as some peddlers did. Clearly he
was innocent. But who then had done it?

Sidney thought fleetingly of that other bed in the far
corner of the hayloft. That was the corner where the
smoke was billowing out most thickly. Someone else had
been in the barn this night!

At that moment a clanging and rattling and thundering
of hooves could be heard way up on the highway. In the
gray light of early dawn, just as everything was beginning
to look hopeless, the Foreston fire wagon came whirling
down the hill. Several men in yellow oilskins stood along
its sides, ready to jump off the moment it stopped.

Though Sidney had seen motorized fire engines in Chicago on many occasions, he found this sight more thrilling.
The big red wagon with shiny brass fittings, the galloping
black horses, the brave-looking men standing ready—all
together it was the most exciting vehicle he had ever seen.

Sidney and the peddler stood watching in admiration.
The little group of men around the barn set up a hoarse
cheer. Karl threw a pail of water in the air and it showered
over him, but in his exuberance he did not seem to notice.
Mama and Elizabeth ran out and stood watching from the
porch as the fire fighters went into action. The blackened
faces of Papa and the neighbors showed their relief. The
battle was out of their hands now.

The Barn Is On Fire!

The hose men quickly uncoiled the hose, fastening it to the pump. A kind of extension rod was put on the pump handle, and all the men took up their stations and went to work. Two men pumped while others carried and directed the hose. Still others attacked the scattered small flames with a new kind of cylinder-shaped fire extinguisher filled with chemicals. Together they made a kind of human machine, each one functioning as an individual part. Sidney observed that the pump handle moved as fast as the Larsen's when driven by the windmill in a strong wind.

"They will win yet—you'll see!" cried the Laugh Peddler admiringly. He was looking almost happy again, forgetting his own grievance for the moment.

And win they did! When the sun rose on the eastern horizon, the barn still stood. There were huge burned-out holes in the siding, and blackened, burned-off timbers, plus a great gaping hole in the floor of the hayloft. The horse stable partitions and stalls were burned away, but the barn walls remained.

The damage was indeed serious, but temporary repairs could be made to make the barn usable through the winter. And next summer more extensive repairs could be done. A farmer had to be a makeshift carpenter almost every day of his life, and that was what was needed now.

"With a bit of work and new lumber, that barn can be fixed up pretty good," said the Laugh Peddler to Sidney as they walked around surveying the damage. "Then next summer it can be made better than ever."

The hay was the biggest loss; it was a huge charred mass now. Sidney remembered how hard Papa and Karl had worked last summer to put it up, and how pleased Pa had looked as he wiped his sweaty face on his sleeve and jumped off the last load. "First time I ever got all the hay in without getting it rained on and having to spread it out at least once," he'd said. Now that precious hay was a useless black mass that would have to be pitched out and destroyed.

But the hayrack and all the tools were saved. And the walls of the barn stood, and neither the stock nor the horses were lost. As Mama said, "We can be thankful when misfortune strikes and still leaves us so much."

6. What Is Wrong with Karl?

Mama invited everyone in for coffee and sandwiches and doughnuts, so after a while the tired men began trooping into the kitchen. They ate and drank with gusto; even Elizabeth's clumsily made emergency sandwiches melted away.

"A fire burns the strength right out of your body," said the fire chief. "Seems as though I am always most hungry after I've fought a fire—especially when we've won!"

Everyone remarked how lucky it was that the peddler had been sleeping in the barn. "I doubt you'd still have a barn—or any stock or horses—if the peddler hadn't been in there to give an early alarm. A bit of luck I'd say," said one of the men, looking over at Yusef Hanna.

Papa did not answer. He did not even glance at the peddler, who stood alone in a corner drinking his coffee. The neighbors, too, seemed to avoid looking at him. All of them showed more or less openly that they, like Papa, believed him responsible for the fire.

Only the fire department men, whose job was to put out fires and not to determine causes, gave him credit for preventing a total loss. They fought many fires and knew that though a farmer always looked for other causes, the blame could often be laid to some carelessness on his own part.

Sidney went over to Karl, who was pulling his socks off beside the stove, but Karl moved away. "Got awful wet," he said shortly. "I'm going upstairs to change."

Sidney followed him to the stairway, planting himself on the lowest step as Karl tried to push past him. "There was someone else sleeping in the hayloft, wasn't there?" he asked, looking into Karl's eyes earnestly. "I mean in the place where your coat was, in the far corner. That's where the fire started, I'm sure."

Karl answered gruffly, almost under his breath. "I don't know nothing about it. Maybe you saw my coat—what of it? I get warm working in the barn and take off my coat sometimes and throw it down where I happen to be."

"What's the matter with you anyway?" Sidney was puzzled and angry, for Karl had pushed him out of the way roughly and was leaping up the stairs two at a time. Sidney heard him slam his door upstairs. It would be useless to try to get anything out of him now, but tomorrow he would go

after him again. The truth was bound to come out, with or without Karl's help. When it did, Sidney was sure it would show that the Laugh Peddler was not responsible for the fire.

Papa and Mama were thanking the neighbors for their help. The men were going home to do their own chores, thankful that they still had barns to do them in.

They spoke in low tones together a few minutes, then Mr. Larsen cleared his throat as if beginning a speech. "We want to say," he began, "that you're not to worry, Fred, about how you're going to feed your stock and such. We know how high hay is this year and how hard it would be for you to buy right now needing all you have to fix up the barn. Well, all of us have a little more hay than we'll use; some others in the community, too. Among us, we can let you have a load or two as you need it. That way we'll see you through the winter. And the horses—why, you can stable them in my barn until you get your own in shape. I can make room for them and feed and water them with my own, or Karl can come over each day and do it if you like. Main thing is they'll have shelter. You'd do the same thing for me, I know."

Papa could hardly speak for gratitude. Mama kept wiping her eyes, smiling tremulously. Their gratitude at having the barn saved had been overshadowed by the fear that they would have to sell their cows, lacking hay to feed them.

There were only the repairs to the barn to worry about

now. Papa said he would begin right away in the morning. One of the neighbors had already told him he had some extra lumber lying around that he would be glad to sell him at cost. It would save him a much longer trip to the nearest lumberyard. With so much neighborly help offered, it would not be long before everything would be nearly normal again.

The fire department men took one more careful look around to be sure that nothing was still smoldering. They advised Papa to keep wetting down the charred places all day so no new blaze could flare up from hidden embers. Then they climbed aboard their wagon, and with a victorious flourish whirled out of the yard.

And so, quite suddenly, everything was quiet again. Papa called Karl to get the cows back into the still usable lower barn, warning him to be gentle so as not to affect the milking.

"They're likely to be skittery from the prodding with the pitchfork a while ago," grumbled Karl. "Anything I do now won't make any difference. I may not even be able to get them back in."

Mama told Sidney to bring in wood and water, then he and Elizabeth must hurry and get washed for breakfast, so they could start for school on time.

Sidney protested vigorously that he should not have to go to school today. There were things like the barn repairs he might be able to help with. But Mama said Papa had not indicated he would be needed. Then seeing his crestfallen face, she added reassuringly, "He may want you to help on Saturday."

As they walked to school, Sidney and Elizabeth talked about the fire. Both were convinced it was not the Laugh Peddler who had started it.

In the hurry of getting ready for school, Sidney had forgotten him, but Elizabeth said she had seen him sitting in the cold " front room" arranging his pack just before she left the house. "He looked kind of sad, I thought. He didn't even notice me. He wasn't at all the way he usually is."

"I'm sure Karl knows something he isn't telling," said Sidney sagely. He stopped and stood thinking as he whacked at a patch of milkweed with his lunch pail. A few late pods, not yet opened fully, released their seeds under the beating and the silky whiteness flew up like snow. "I'll make him tell what he knows about that other bed in the hayloft. I know he knows something about the whole business, something that would clear the Laugh Peddler, if he will talk."

"I've noticed he's been acting funny lately," said Elizabeth. "He's real cranky sometimes, like something's bothering him that he can't talk about. He must have some kind of bad secret."

"You bet he does!" said Sidney. "And I'm going to find out what it is tonight. This time he won't put me off either."

It was an exciting day at school. With Christmas drawing

near, there was important planning for decorations, and program practice began. Before the nine o'clock bell rang, however, both Sidney and Elizabeth found themselves the centers of attention because of the fire, and they enjoyed their role as firsthand storytellers.

But soon classes and Christmas preparations and playground fun absorbed their interest. It was not until school was dismissed and they were walking home that they suddenly remembered their contract with the Laugh Peddler.

"We'll give him the money tonight—after we get the wood, so we have the whole dollar," said Sidney. "My parents sometimes paid a dollar down on things; it's a good start. One dollar down and owing him three—that's not bad. If I can earn some money during vacation, and you get some for Christmas, we'll have them paid for."

"You could almost say we've done it already," said Elizabeth. "It's going to be the best surprise for Mama! She hasn't got the least idea."

7. The Laugh Peddler Is Gone

They set their lunch pails on the kitchen table and sniffed the air. "Pumpkin pie!" exclaimed Sidney. "And that good smell coming from the oven must be baked beans. The Laugh Peddler will just love this supper!"

Mama came out of the pantry where she had set the pies out to cool. "The Laugh Peddler is gone," she said. "He left this morning, and he won't be coming back."

The children stared at her, hardly able to take in what she was saying. It was plain that Mama was unhappy about it, too. Something was very wrong. "Then you won't get the pretty dress silk," Elizabeth said slowly.

"Oh, yes, he'd given that to me the first thing, you know, and he wouldn't take it back. I didn't want to keep it; it wasn't nearly paid for with meals. I feel so bad about the whole thing."

The Laugh Peddler gone! To the children the world had suddenly fallen apart. Aside from the fact that he was such wonderful company, there were the combs that were supposed to be Mama's Christmas present. All their fine planning had come to nothing.

Mama told them about the quarrel between Papa and Yusef Hanna. Later that morning the subject of the fire had come up again. Once more the peddler had affirmed his innocence, insisting that he had not smoked in the hayloft. "I awoke smelling smoke," he said, "but I had not touched a match out there. I did not start that fire. And I do not lie—you ought to know that! I've been coming here so long."

But Papa had only looked skeptical and answered, "All I know is that it started in the hayloft and you were the one sleeping there. If not you, who else could have done it?"

The argument went back and forth, even though Mama tried to make peace and smooth things over. Finally Yusef Hanna had said he thought it best to leave. He did not want to stay in a house where his word was doubted. And of course now he could no longer sleep in the barn anyway, though Mama had offered to fix up a couch for him in the kitchen. He thanked her, but strapped on his pack and said good-by, following the road down to the highway.

Sidney knew what he must do. He changed his clothes quickly and went out to the barn. There he found Papa at work in the horse stable, hacking out burned timbers. Sidney sat down and waited until Papa stopped to rest for a moment. He was no longer afraid of Papa's impatience; this was too important a matter.

"I don't think the Laugh Peddler started the fire," he began. "I happen to know that someone else had a bed in the hayloft. I came across it yesterday when I went to search for a hen's nest. I was going to tell you last night, but you went out so fast. Karl hurried us up—remember? I think he knows something he isn't telling."

Papa had listened carefully, then went back to his work. "I know how you feel about Yusef Hanna and understand that you want to protect him," he said. "But your arguments are not convincing. Karl could have fixed himself a little hideaway in the hay. Nothing wrong with that. But we know he doesn't smoke, and anyway he sleeps in the house nights. As much as I go in and out of the barn at all hours, I'd certainly have seen if anyone was there."

"But the bed was over in the far corner," said Sidney stubbornly. "And Karl always threw down the hay. And what if the someone who slept there was careful to come into the barn late every night and leave before anyone was up in the morning? No one would see him then."

Sidney was sure he was right, but he realized it was against all rules to talk to parents this way, and Papa was not just any parent, either. There was no use going on; Papa had made it plain that he was too busy to listen and was not greatly concerned about the matter, either.

"All signs point to the peddler," he said with finality, sinking his crowbar into a charred board and prying it out. "I won't hear any more about it now. And you don't need to worry about the peddler. He'll be back next spring with another load of goods to sell. They're a tough lot—peddlers —they'll do anything to avoid doing real man's work. He'll be back—don't worry."

"I don't think so," said Sidney, turning away. "Maybe other peddlers are like you say, but Yusef Hanna is different. He feels bad about things just like anyone else. He felt very bad about the fire. And he shouldn't have to take the blame when—"

"Well, we'll ask Karl about it tonight," said Papa, tearing at half-burned boards. "He's over at Larsen's now helping to make room for our horses. Don't bother me any more; I still have to go after that lumber. Go see if there's anything you can do in the house."

Sidney turned away and walked to the house in low spirits. After yesterday's conversation with Papa, he'd thought it might be different talking to him, but the situation was the same as always. He had screwed up his courage to talk to him in a man-to-man way, only to be put off as if his words and arguments were hardly worth listening to. Tears of angry frustration came into his eyes, remembering the big, long talks he used to have with his real father in Chicago.

"Is that so, Sidney, my boy?" Daddy would say when Sidney was telling him something, looking into Sidney's eyes with interest. "That's the way you see it, eh? Well, old man, maybe you have something there. Yessir, now I think about it, I believe you may be right!" And then they would discuss the question from all sides until Sidney would grow tired and want to stop. Talking with Daddy had really been *talking*.

Elizabeth had been sent to bring in some wood, and they went into the woodshed together and filled their arms with stove lengths. They talked sadly of the loss of their hopes of giving Mama a present, and they were both angry at Papa. But they conceded that he could not be blamed entirely, either.

Papa did not know the Laugh Peddler as they did. And he had all those harsh ideas about working—as if farmwork were the only real work there was in the world, and as if being a peddler was a silly, unimportant job with no dignity to it. And now he was extra worried because of all it would cost to fix up the barn. It was not safe the way it was; that was why he was in such furious haste to make the repairs.

But they could not forget that he had been unfair to the Laugh Peddler. He had driven him away, and in spite of what Papa had said to Sidney about the toughness of peddlers, they doubted that he would ever come back again. That thought was almost unendurable.

They piled the wood neatly in the woodbox and sat around the kitchen disconsolately. Mama sent them into the dining room with the twins, so she could get a bit of ironing done. Sidney took the Funston Fur Company catalog and showed the animal pictures to Ernest. He noted that muskrat pelts had gone up in price.

Papa had mentioned once that trapping might be something Sidney could do to earn a little extra money, as soon as the lake froze over. Sidney was not sure he'd like that way of getting ahead, though Papa pointed out that it was easy, requiring no special skill or strength. He had showed him the traps in the woodshed when he'd talked to him about the beaver colony. Again and again he mentioned how he prized those beavers and how glad he was that they enjoyed protection at last.

There were only a few beaver colonies in the state, and even they would soon have been gone if the law had not passed. Here and there in remote areas where they had escaped the notice of trappers, you could find them, in spite of the merciless trapping that had gone on for over a hundred years. In the East they had already disappeared. That was why Sidney must be careful not to talk about the beavers, except to those already in on the secret. Larry, of course, was one of those, since his father had also worked to get the protection bill passed.

Sidney liked both the beavers and the muskrats, though the latter were common and plentiful. Their brown houses made the edge of the lake ugly in summer. But still, Sidney did not think it would be very pleasant work to have to trap them. He thought he would rather find some other way to earn money.

The Laugh Peddler Is Gone

Elizabeth was amusing Ellen by changing her doll bed. The bed was a large wicker basket and the doll lived and slept in it. Mama had given her some little squares of sheeting so she would be able to make it up like a real bed.

As she lifted off the doll blanket and picked up her doll, a pasteboard box fell out. It looked strangely familiar. Her eyes grew bright with excitement as she picked it up. It was the one box she had been dreaming of ever since the peddler had tucked it away at the bottom of his pack.

Elizabeth quickly hid it from the twins. When they were busy in the corner she whispered, "Sidney, look!" She opened the box and there, in all their loveliness, were the rhinestone combs!

In the bottom of the box was a note: "I leave the combs for you so you have them for your Mama's present. You pay me when you can. Yusef Hanna."

"He remembered! He remembered after all! Oh, he's a good, good Laugh Peddler—a true friend!"

She held the box lovingly in her hands. The combs were even more beautiful than she had remembered.

"Sh—sh!" warned Sidney. "Don't let—you know—see —or you know!" He edged closer and studied the hiding place the peddler had chosen. "It's just like him—still trying to cheer us up when he's unhappy himself. All we have to do now is send him the down payment.

"And say—I almost forgot! Pa said yesterday we could go over to the island and look at the beavers—then bring a load of firewood and he'd pay us for it. In the excitement of the fire and everything I didn't think of it till now. We can make that quarter and send the dollar—our first payment—off tomorrow. There's still time to go. They just drove off to get the lumber, and that will take an hour at least. Supper will probably be a little late tonight. Even if it's a bit dark coming back, we know our way. Let's go!"

8. To the Island!

They dressed quickly and hurried off, heading first for the lakeshore woods. They pulled the clumsy, homemade sled behind them, but the under layer of snow had hardened, so it glided along easily. It had begun to snow again and was growing colder.

Doogan started to follow, but they sent him home. At his age a trip like this would be exhausting for him and would slow them down. "Go home, Doog," shouted Sidney. "We'll soon be back." The old sheep dog turned obediently and went home.

Just beyond the lakeshore woods—a few hundred feet out from the sandy bay that was their swimming place in summer—loomed the island, a gray-green mass on the snow-swept lake. After Papa's story, it could have only one name to them. It would be Treasure Island from now on.

"Are you sure the ice is safe?" asked Elizabeth. It appeared that she was already tired and would willingly have postponed the trip. Sidney, however, was more eager than ever to go on. He pretended not to notice her weariness.

"Of course, it's safe," he said confidently. "You know what Larry said. Your Pa never would have let us go unless he was sure, too."

They turned outward from the shore, heading directly across the lake toward the island. They found it heavier going now for the new snow was piling thickly here. They were following deep depressions which, though filling with snow, showed clearly as large footprints. These were helpful as a track to follow and for a while Sidney paid little attention to them. Suddenly he stopped short, looking puzzled.

"That's funny," he said. "Who in the world could have made these tracks? I didn't think about it at first, but look—they go straight to the island! Who'd be going there anyway? They're so big they couldn't be Larry's. And they must have been made yesterday, after it snowed."

Elizabeth stood still, unable to offer an explanation. She seemed glad of a chance to rest and catch her breath. It was beginning to snow harder now, and the wind was rising. The children pulled at their stocking caps and scarves to protect ears and faces better.

"We'll just take a quick look at the beavers and the shack,

and get our load of wood and go back," said Sidney. "There won't be so much snow on the island because of the trees, so it won't take long." His face was red and pinched, and his eyes looked worried in spite of his brave talk. "We'll find out who made those tracks when we get home. It might turn out to be Karl—or even Pa."

But he remembered the hours of work on the stock shelter yesterday and today's labor on the barn repairs, and knew that it was highly improbable that either of them had taken time for a walk on the lake. Besides, Pa would have mentioned it, he was sure.

The tracks became more numerous on the island. They went in all directions, in and out of the woods. The steadily falling snow added to the feeling of mystery that had begun to envelop them both.

They found themselves shivering, and it was not altogether from the cold. The island in a snow storm was quite different from the way it looked in summer. It was more than a little scary now in the gathering dusk. They walked warily, avoiding the snow-shrouded forms of trees that seemed to both warn and beckon. The wind moaned in the white stillness.

"It's certainly more cheerful here in summer," said Sidney. "There are birds around then, and it isn't so quiet. I didn't think it would be so different, or I wouldn't have been so anxious to come."

They pushed through the overhanging branches of the pines toward the shack standing at the center of the island.

Sidney felt a tightening in his stomach as they drew near it on the narrow trail. Something always clutched him there when he felt afraid.

Elizabeth's look showed plainly that she, too, was frightened. "My legs are getting tired," she said. "I wish I hadn't come. I don't like this island a bit. But you'll get us home soon, won't you, Sidney?"

"Of course, I'll get you home!" Sidney was purposely cheerful and hid his own fear. He hadn't realized how far it was and how quickly it grew dark in winter. And there were those unexplained footprints.

They came on the shack suddenly. It stood crowded into a small open space, pressed on all sides by towering trees. They stopped in their tracks, staring in unbelief, for it was no longer a play shack. A litter of traps, tools, and tin cans was scattered near the doorway, and though snow was sifting over everything softly, there was no mistaking what this meant. The strange footprints led straight to the door which was hung with a blanket from inside.

"Someone's living here!" said Sidney, breathing hard. He took off his mitten and rubbed his hand across his eyes. "Someone is using our shack—to trap from. Look at those traps! Who in the world?"

Then they saw the furs. Strung around the outside walls of the shack was a heavy wire from which hung rows of pelts. Each skin was on a thin wooden shingle, a pelt-stretcher, like those they'd seen muskrat trappers use. The fur side was turned in, but wherever edges of it showed, it

was rich beaver brown in color, unlike the tawny shades of muskrat skins.

"Beaver!" whispered Sidney. "Someone is trapping our beavers! And just look how many! Who'd dare to anyway? They're protected by law and there's a heavy fine just for killing one beaver."

Papa had told him how hopeful he was that this colony would grow to be a large one in a few years, one from which other colonies could be started. Now here was their own—at least it seemed their own—secretly protected colony cold-bloodedly slaughtered!

Elizabeth shivered with horror. "It must be somebody terribly mean to do such a thing," she whispered, clutching Sidney's hand and holding on to it tightly. "They'll go to jail, won't they?"

"Don't worry," said Sidney. "That's what a game warden is for. Mr. Wold will be coming around one of these days, and Pa will tell him about this. He'll go after the poacher, whoever he is. That mean killer will get what's coming to him—just wait and see!"

He studied the evidence around the shack and examined the stiff skins carefully. "I just hate to tell Pa, though! He's been so proud of this beaver colony and he seemed to think they were so perfectly safe here. But he did say that this county is too big a territory; the game warden doesn't get around as often as he should. Now this proves he was right. But who in the world could have discovered the beavers in this hidden place? Who?"

To The Island!

Sidney and Elizabeth moved slowly toward the doorway, which was hung with a gray horse blanket that Sidney was sure came from their own barn. Inside, a rank odor hung in the cold air. There was a faint smell of a recent fire from one corner of the shack evidently used as a fireplace. A black pot lay nearby with coffee grounds in its bottom, and a skillet lay in the ashes.

The grass "floor" of the shack had long been trampled into dirt in the center area near the huge board-topped stump that Sidney and Larry had built the shack around and used as a table. Now it was evidently being used for one purpose only—as a place to skin beavers. Two blood-caked knives lay on it, and it was streaked with blood down to the ground. Obviously the shack was someone's trapping base, and he was also cooking meals here, for the ashes in the fireplace were still warm. The two wooden boxes that Sidney and Larry had brought over for "chairs" still stood in one corner.

"It's a poacher's hideout," said Sidney. "He ate his dinner here not long ago. But he isn't sleeping here; there's no place except the ground, and that would be too cold. Do you suppose—I'll bet he's the one that was sleeping in our barn! Remember the footprints; they came from our side of the lake."

Elizabeth's eyes were panic-stricken. Her teeth chattered as she looked around the shack. "Please, Sidney, let's get out of here! Let's run home and tell Papa! He'll know what to do."

To the Island!

Sidney studied the stump carefully. "You bet we'll tell him! Now maybe I can make him believe that it wasn't the Laugh Peddler who started the fire last night. Whoever hauled this horse blanket out here has been in our barn, and you can bet he was the one made that other bed in the hay. Pa will be sorry now for blaming the Laugh Peddler. But he'll see to it that the game warden hears about this right away. You can be sure he'll know what to do."

"Oh, will he now?" A raspy voice spoke suddenly from the doorway. There a tall, loose-limbed man with a dark bearded face, topped by a sheepskin cap, stood holding up a corner of the blanket door. He came inside slowly, dropping two dead beavers on the ground as he did so.

Surprise and fear held the children speechless. The stranger appeared the very embodiment of the vague evil they had sensed since they set foot on the island. Elizabeth crowded close to Sidney as he put a protective arm around her. He stared back at the poacher with a boldness he was far from feeling.

"Who are you?" he asked. "This is our shack—mine and Larry Larsen's. You had no right to move in like this!"

The stranger made him a mocking bow. "Ah—owner of thees fine house, eh? Let me introduce polite." His darkened teeth showed in a sudden crooked smile. He stepped closer, looking down into their upturned faces, and they stepped back, right into the fireplace ashes.

"Well, maybe you hear of Pete Marlin, eh? Farm hand and odd-jobs man around here since last spring...."

They both nodded. They knew there had been such a man in the community; some of their schoolmates had mentioned him now and then. He worked a few weeks here and a few weeks there, mostly for farmers. In between, he worked around the dock at Marine Landing, at any job offered. No one knew exactly where he came from; some thought Canada, since he often spoke of "up nort."

Pete Marlin's face assumed a mock humility now. "No tink much of Pete, eh? Just bum for do work on farm an' dock. But up nort—upriver from Bois Brule on border—there *Trapper* Pete! Good trapper too—take all kinds of skins and get good money." He drew himself up proudly. "Not like here where only farms. Up nort, trapping is real beeg job!"

"It's illegal to trap beaver in this state, you know," said Sidney. His first fear had left him, and he was filled mostly with indignation. "You're in for a big fine, mister. You might even go to jail when you're caught!"

"Ah, but Pete never be caught," said the trapper. He took out a pouch of smoking tobacco and cigarette papers, and began rolling a cigarette skillfully. "I don't tink you little ones tell what you see."

Both Sidney and Elizabeth had observed that he was wearing Karl's sheepskin coat—the one Sidney had seen beside the mysterious hayloft bed. It confirmed Sidney's suspicions completely. "You were in our barn hayloft last night. It was your bed I saw in the corner, and it was you started the fire!"

The trapper smiled slightly. "Could be," he said. "I'm used to sleep in barn; hayloft make pretty good bed. Shack too cold. And your hen lay fine eggs too—make good omelets. Good place all right. Too bad it burn."

His expression changed suddenly and became menacing. "You farm brats," he growled. "Why you come poking in here, when everyting going good? Now I must clear out—make for border fast...

"But good you bring me sled. A real favor to Pete. No need now to go steal one to carry all my pelts." He smiled.

Sidney stood uncertain and silent. It was getting darker outside, and he began to fear that they might actually be in some danger. Best get out as quickly as possible. He began pulling Elizabeth toward the door, and the poacher made no move to stop them.

As they ducked under the blanket door he could not resist the temptation to get off a last defiant word. "You'll be sorry you killed our beavers," he shouted. "You're sure to be caught!"

Elizabeth added her small threat too. "You're a real mean man, and you'll be sorry when we tell on you!"

The trapper crossed in two long steps to where they stood. He seized Elizabeth by the shoulders and held her in a vise-like grip. His face was so close that they could smell the tobacco and stale fish on his breath.

"I'm warning—you no tell!" The poacher spoke with quiet menace. "You keep secret! If you tell before Pete make getaway to border—if Pete caught—I come back burn barn again. And this time would be no accident from cigarette—no! I would see it burn to ground—cows, horses, everyting!" He blew a puff of smoke into their faces and laughed as they ducked.

"Let's get out of here!" Sidney put both his arms around Elizabeth and pulled her along. Outside, safely on the trail, he called back, "Someone's sure to see you even if we don't tell. You'll be caught with the skins somewhere on the road."

The trapper stood leaning against the shed and did not bother to answer. With dark coming on he had little to fear. He could get to the Landing easily in time to catch the early morning boat. No one on a freight boat would inquire about the contents of his big box, and his threats to the children would keep them quiet. He had calculated swiftly and well.

As the trees hid the shack from view they heard him call a final warning, "I never come back here! All my life I no come back. No good place. Farmers, phui! But you no tell! If you do—pouf!"

9. The Blizzard Strikes

The children ran blindly, stumbling against trees and gasping with fright at his threat. It had grown almost dark, and the falling snow had changed from large soft flakes into a swirling powdery whiteness. The moan of the wind had turned into a thin wailing in the high pine branches. It was steadily growing colder.

"I *will* tell just the same," Sidney panted. "They'll catch him and put him in jail and he can't do anything to our barn then. Those threats don't scare me."

"But what if he gets out of jail? He will some time you know," sobbed Elizabeth. "He might come back then and do it. Oh, no, we mustn't tell! We mustn't tell, Sidney. Please don't!"

They were out of the island woods and onto the lake now. The full force of the icy wind struck them here. It was laden with fine, sharp snow that cut their faces like slanting needles. It pushed at them like a human physical force, and though they struggled against it bravely, they made little headway.

"I never thought the weather could turn so quick," said Sidney. The viciousness of the storm bewildered him; he had never experienced a country blizzard though he had heard about such storms. "It'll be easier once we get to the shore. This is like the blizzard Pa told about, the one he was caught in after he came to this country."

Elizabeth was unable to answer; she was struggling valiantly to hold her own, but found it hard to breathe. The gale was so fierce that it seemed actually to suck the breath out of her mouth.

Sidney turned to look at her closely for a moment. He wondered what he could do to shield her. He recalled Papa's words as he had described that awful blizzard he had experienced, and the life-saving techniques he had learned, which he had passed on to those listening:

"You should wrap something around your lower face when you begin to find it hard to breathe. Maybe you can only find a twist of long grass, but you should get something over your mouth so you can keep the breath in your body. Then if you can't get your directions in all that churning whiteness, look for something to follow—a fence or a ditch. If there are trees around, you can nearly always get your bearings by feeling which side of the tree has snow plastered against it. That'll most likely be the north side. And never sit down to rest—never! Keep moving whatever you do."

Papa's words came back to Sidney now as he realized he must help Elizabeth. Quickly he unwrapped the scarf from Elizabeth's neck and began wrapping it around the lower part of her face until her mouth and nose were covered with several layers of loosely knit wool, shielding her breathing from the fierce suction of the wind. He took off his own short scarf and placed it over his mouth and nose, tying it tightly behind. He found that it made breathing easier. They went on against the buffeting wind and at last reached the shelter of the wooded shore.

But where were they? They had not traveled in a straight line and now it was quite dark; the eerie twilight of swirling snow had suddenly become terrifying blackness. Sidney found it impossible to get his bearings.

Holding tightly to Elizabeth, he walked a short distance in each direction, trying to find something familiar. He knew their own shore woods fairly well, but everything was strange in this whirling darkness.

They huddled against a tree for a moment's protection and Sidney felt around its trunk. From the very smooth feel of its bark he thought it might be a birch—maybe one of the large birches in that little copse right down by the lake. If it was one of those, he knew they would be close to the fence that separated their land from Larsen's.

"This is the birch copse, I'm sure—there's another smooth tree right next to this one," he said to Elizabeth. "Then we're on our land and the fence that follows our farm line is to the north. The snow is plastered heaviest on the right side of this tree, so that must be the north side. If I go toward the right, then maybe we'll get to our fence and we can follow that to the drainage ditch. We'll follow that to the slough, and then we'll be almost right home."

Elizabeth no longer seemed to have strength to answer. She sank against the tree like a grain sack.

Papa had added another bit of advice about blizzard survival, almost as an afterthought, and it came back to Sidney now: "If you're with anyone, don't let yourselves get separated—not even by a few feet. You can't see and hear any distance, so if you should get separated, you'd not find each other again. Best thing is to tie yourselves together with anything you happen to have on you. Erik had a piece of binder twine in his pocket, and he used that to tie us together in the '88 blizzard. I was only fifteen at the time, new to the country. That bit of twine may have saved my life."

To search for the fence, probably only a few feet away, and at the same time to keep from getting separated—that was the problem. He had nothing in the way of a cord. "I could just as well have had that hank of twine in the woodshed," he reflected ruefully. He had meant to bring it to tie down the wood they were to gather on the sled, but in the hurry to get started he had forgotten.

But suddenly he had a solution. "My scarf! I'll have to spare it."

He spoke encouragingly to Elizabeth, explaining what he was about to do, then pulled off his short wool scarf, ripped it down the middle to make a long heavy band. With this he lashed her right wrist to his own left, tying it securely. They were inseparable now.

He could safely search for the fence now and he began to reach out with his free right hand, hoping somehow to come upon the familiar wire as they stumbled forward. They fell repeatedly against logs and stumps, but Sidney's strength was equal to pulling both of them up each time. Finally it seemed simpler just to crawl on hands and knees, he slightly ahead, feeling his way forward with his free right hand. He was aware neither of cold or fear now. He knew that their lives depended on finding that fence.

Suddenly his hand closed on something solid and up-right. Swiftly he pushed off his mitten so as to examine it better. There was no bark so it could not be a tree. His fingers moved upward eagerly and touched barbed wire. It was a fence post. They had found the fence!

"Cheer up, Liz'beth!" he cried into her ear. "We're not lost any more! We're at our own fence now!"

He hugged her and shook her, for she had fallen flat and lay without movement in the snow. Her only reply was a moan. He knew that she must be almost spent; she probably was worn out even before they got to the island. Sidney knew now that he could battle the storm and make it home. But he did not have only himself to think about; he must get Elizabeth home, too. And how could she hold out?

"Please, Liz'beth," he begged earnestly. "Don't give up now! It's not much farther—really! We'll follow the fence to the ditch and then follow the ditch, and we'll be there."

She struggled to her feet. He began pulling her along behind him as his free hand carefully followed the barbed wire. If her strength just held out for this much movement, they'd make it.

But pulling her was becoming harder. It was apparent that she could not go much farther even with his strong help. He wondered desperately what to do. She had fallen flat again, and he sank down beside her in the snow, one hand still holding to the fence. He must think of a way to keep her moving. Papa's grim warning echoed in his ears: "Never, never sit down to rest in a blizzard! They'll be straightening you out for a coffin, if you do."

"Come on, Liz'beth," he pleaded, pulling at her arm. Then putting his left arm around her, he tried to lift her to her feet. But there was no answer now; the small form lay still.

Sidney clutched the barbed wire until he felt a sting of pain through his mitten. He *had* to get her up again! At that moment something large and firm closed over his hand. Peering down, he saw that it was the mittened hand of a man. He heard a voice shout in his ear: "Thank God, I found you!" It was the Laugh Peddler.

Sidney let go of the fence then, and threw his free arm around the stocky frame of Yusef Hanna, hugging him tightly. He could feel tears freezing on his eyelashes, but they were tears of joy and relief. He could not find words to express what he felt. He pulled the peddler down to where Elizabeth still lay, as he loosened the rag that bound them together. Yusef Hanna immediately picked her up in his arms, saying, "Poor child! Don't worry now. I'll take over; I'll get you home."

Sidney began to explain, shouting to make himself heard: "I was following the fence to the ditch. It must be close; we're going downhill now. Liz'beth just couldn't go on any longer...."

In the arms of the Laugh Peddler, she revived quickly, however. She accepted the fact of his sudden appearance as natural.

"We'll just take it slow and easy," said the Laugh Peddler soothingly. "Stay close behind, Sidney, and we'll find that ditch. The wind is not so bad now."

The ditch, dug only last summer in order to drain the slough, was very familiar to Sidney. He had brought water to the men as they worked and had watched the long tiles being laid. "I know just where it comes into the slough," he said. "It's below the apple orchard. And the trees are in rows; we can follow them easy to the house."

Suddenly they found themselves pitched forward, almost falling on their faces. They had found the ditch. There was protection from the wind here, and the walking was easier. They made good headway and were at the orchard when they were met by the dear shaggy form of Doogan. He was followed by Papa, who quickly took Elizabeth from the peddler's arms. The little procession, safe at last, made its way to the house, with Doogan leading the way.

10. Home Again at Last

Soon the whole frozen party tumbled into the kitchen. No place had ever looked more beautiful to Sidney than the lamp-lighted kitchen with its big black stove pouring out welcome warmth.

Mama had spread blankets on the floor and now began pulling off their clothes as she hugged them and cried over them by turns. Papa brought in a basin of snow and together they began rubbing the faces and arms and legs of the children.

"Are you really safe?" cried Mama. "Is it true? I was afraid—"

The Laugh Peddler was using a handful of snow to rub hard at a white spot on his swarthy cheek as he stood before the mirror above the sink. He said reassuringly that the worst they had to deal with was frostbite, and it would yield quickly to the first aid with snow. "I've had my ears and cheeks frostbitten so many times I've lost count," he said cheerfully. "But a little snow brings back the color fast, and all you have is a bit of prickling. No pain."

"We weren't really lost," Sidney managed to say through stiff lips. "It was only that we were getting so awful tired. The Laugh Peddler found us just in time."

Papa and the Laugh Peddler were talking earnestly as they continued to peel off clothing and pull icicles out of their hair and whiskers. "I would have gone after them right away myself, except I had gone after that lumber for the barn. Karl was along, too, and we had trouble just getting home ourselves. I knew we were in for it soon as the wind hit in that sudden way. I just hoped the children hadn't gone across the lake. I started out to find them soon as I heard."

"And you did; you did all you could," said the peddler, holding his hands over the stove to warm them.

"I wouldn't have found them soon enough to have done any good, I'm afraid. If you hadn't been in the woods—I don't dare think what might have happened!"

"This boy has a head on his shoulders," said the Laugh Peddler, taking no notice of Papa's words. "He knows enough not to stay lost. For a boy raised in the city, he did real well in a blizzard. Seems like he's picked up some country wisdom already."

"How did you happen to be coming through the woods?" asked Papa. "You weren't caught in the storm, were you?"

"Well, no; not exactly," answered the peddler. "See, being on the road so much, a man gets to know storm signs. I was planning on getting the 5:45 train from Cove Pass, and I was heading east on that road about mid-afternoon when I felt the wind swing around to the north. With snow in the air, I knew that meant trouble. So I just headed for Larsen's, a couple of miles back, you know. He'd told me last night, or this morning really, that I was welcome to come there and stay till I finished my selling. So with a storm coming up, that seemed a good idea. Mrs. Larsen was home alone; he and the boy were off butchering. And, well, she happened to have seen your children going across the lake earlier and she told me about it. We didn't see how they'd make it back when the storm struck so fierce. I couldn't sit there and not try to find them; I had to go—do what I could...." His voice drifted off almost apologetically.

"You'd have gone way to the island to find us?" asked Sidney.

"I guess so," said Yusef Hanna softly. "But as it turned out, I didn't need to. Now you tell me something. How did you ever find that fence? It was all I could do to find it from Larsen's house."

"Well, see, I figured by the feel of the bark on the tree first. I could tell it was a birch, so I was sure we must be in that little white copse on the lake shore. Then I remembered what Pa had said about finding the north side of a tree; it's where the snow is plastered on the thickest. From that I knew which way to go to get to the fence. And, well, you know the rest."

Elizabeth spoke up admiringly. "He tied us together with his scarf so we wouldn't get separated," she said. "I kept falling down. I was so terribly tired! He saved me—he really did! He kept pulling me up and pulling me up."

Papa ran a rough hand over Sidney's tousled hair and said, "Not many boys your age—not even country boys—would have used their heads so well, or shown such courage. I'm proud of you, Son."

The words were more comforting than the warmth in the kitchen to Sidney. Papa, who seldom spoke words of special kindness or apology, was telling the Laugh Peddler how he could never thank him enough for what he had done and praising him for his courage. He told him, too, how much he regretted his earlier harsh words about the barn fire. Mama echoed his thanks tearfully.

"Well, a blizzard is a terrible thing to be caught in," said Yusef Hanna matter-of-factly. "I've been caught in a few so I know. It's no place for young children, that's sure. The strength of that wind! I couldn't sit still at Larsen's knowing they were out in it."

Mama had gone into the pantry and brought out a jar of goose grease, which she set to heat in a pan on the stove. She poured in a bit of kerosene as it melted, and the strong smell permeated the kitchen. Now she began rubbing the children's legs and feet with it, and here and there where an unnatural spot of red glowed in their faces, she also rubbed in the mixture.

"It's the best country remedy known for frostbite," she explained. "Used in the old country, too, so you know it's good. First you get the circulation back, then you rub in goose grease and kerosene to keep the skin from breaking. Nothing better."

"It stinks!" snapped Elizabeth crossly, turning her head to escape the strong fumes. "I wish you'd stop it! I could get one of my bad headaches from that horrid smell."

Mama only smiled and kept on rubbing, first one child then the other. Their faces glowed rosily now, and the frostbite areas seemed normal again, though a bit red. Papa treated Sidney's scratched hand, where the barbs had pricked through his mitten. "It's a miracle," he said. "A little frostbite and some scratches. And how much worse it could have been!"

He went to the window and looked out. "I'm afraid there will be some folks dying out there tonight. Anyone caught out in this hasn't much chance—unless he finds shelter, of course. You were smart to leave the sled behind; it would have slowed you up."

In the more recent terror of the blizzard, Sidney and Elizabeth had almost forgotten the frightening encounter with Pete Marlin. Pete had not actually threatened their lives as the blizzard had. But now that terrible experience,

with the ominous threat accompanying it, came again to
their minds. They looked at each other guiltily. Neither
said anything in answer, and Elizabeth's eyes were suddenly
wide with fear.

"You went to the island, didn't you?" asked Papa. "And
you had planned to bring back wood, so you must have
had the sled?" He looked from one to the other questioningly, but they were silent.

Mama handed each of them a cup of hot cocoa. It was
very hot, but they drank it. Sidney felt his strength rise with
each swallow. They had won out against the worst enemy
—the storm. Beside that, Pete Marlin seemed small and
puny—even a bit pitiful.

"Do you really mean that people may be dying right
around here? I mean, could it happen to anyone out on the
road, say?"

"If they don't get to some shelter—yes. Why in the
blizzard of '88, four people lost their lives right in our own
neighborhood. One man was lost a few yards from his own
house. If he'd gone ten steps farther in the right direction,
he'd have bumped into it. He'd gone out to the barn to
tend the stock and coming back lost his way and went in
the wrong direction. They could tell how he'd walked in
circles, even gone way out in a field. They found his milk
pail there."

"Well then," said Sidney, drawing a long breath. "I'm
afraid Pete Marlin may be in trouble right now. He may be
lost and dying, unless—"

Papa looked bewildered. "Pete Marlin—what do you know of him?"

"Well, you know he's the man who worked around here this summer and fall, odd jobs, threshing and stuff. I wouldn't have known him myself, but I'd heard about him in school...."

"Yes, yes, I know," said Papa impatiently. "Go on!"

Sidney glanced at Karl who had come in almost unnoticed. He was sitting in the woodbox corner, taking great lumps of snow out of the tops of his woolen socks and throwing them onto the stove where they hissed momentarily and then vanished in clouds of steam. He looked up briefly at Sidney's words.

Sidney looked back at Papa and continued boldly: "Well, we saw Pete Marlin on the island this afternoon. He took the sled away from us, and he was heading for Marine Landing tonight, he said. He must have passed us somewhere in the woods to get to the road, but we didn't see him—not after we left the island." Sidney gulped the last of his cocoa and looked straight at Karl. "He was wearing your sheepskin coat, Karl."

"I sold him the coat," said Karl in a low voice. "But I didn't have anything to do with him. I wasn't—"

"Didn't you know he was using our shack on the island —trapping beavers from there?"

Elizabeth clutched at Sidney's arm. "Don't say anything more, Sidney," she murmured. "You know why you mustn't tell."

But Papa had stood up hastily as if an alarm had gone off. He looked incredulously from Karl to Sidney and back again to Karl. "What's this you're saying? What in the world are you talking about?" he exclaimed angrily. "Trapping our beavers! Are you joking, or what?"

Sidney shook his head. "It's true. We saw the skins, and they were beaver all right. Dozens and dozens of them!"

Papa turned to Karl and spoke with accusing sternness. "If you know anything about this business, you'd better speak up. And don't try to hide anything. I want the whole story, and I want it immediately!"

Karl was looking trapped now himself. He squirmed and stammered uncomfortably for several minutes. But Papa continued to look at him, waiting for Karl to begin his explanation.

Finally Karl cleared his throat nervously. "Aw, I may as well tell, I s'pose. I haven't done anything real wrong, I can tell you that, but I'd just as soon get it off my chest once for all."

Karl began painstakingly to tell of his first encounter with Pete. He had come to the barn late one evening at the end of the threshing season and asked if he might sleep in the barn that night. "I agreed," Karl went on, "and I didn't think just then about your strong objections about smoking around the barn. I guess it was because it was such a pleasure to talk with somebody who was a bit homesick for his native land—Canada—as I was homesick for my own Germany. We sat up talking until late that night, and when I was leaving to come in the house he asked me not to tell anyone he was in the barn. He said he hoped to trap a few muskrat and take the skins back north with him. No one else was trapping, he had observed, and they were so plentiful around lakes here.

"He said that all the farmers believed he'd gone back to Canada, and he wanted it left that way. 'I stay around little longer and make little money,' he said. 'Make up for poor wages and hard work all summer.'

"I pointed out that it was legal to trap muskrat; the season had been open two weeks. But he insisted that, being an outsider like he was, he would be resented as a poacher. It would be much simpler, he said, just to get his fur catch and move on without anyone knowing. He knew a shack in the woods where he could stay during the days, using it as his base of operations, so he'd be in the barn only for sleeping, coming in late at night and going out at sunrise. He'd be no trouble to anyone, he said, so no one need even know he was there.

"I didn't know he was after beaver," Karl insisted. "I did know that he was using the shack on the island, and cooking, and skinning the pelts there. But I thought all the time it was muskrat—why, he even showed me some musk-rat skins he'd taken the first days. I swear I thought that was all he was after! And he kept saying he was moving on in a few days. I just didn't know...."

"I don't see how you could help not knowing!" Papa was very angry now. "It should have sounded fishy to you from the start. Muskrat skins don't bring much; no one would hang around here just for that kind of trapping. And why didn't you speak up after the fire? Why didn't you tell me then that someone else had been sleeping in the barn? You know I wouldn't have blamed Mr. Hanna if I'd known."

"It's this way," said Karl. "He had me trapped—like the beavers, you might say. I found out just yesterday that he had been taking not muskrat, but beaver all this time. It slipped out sort of accidental like. I got mad and told him to get out or I'd tell you. He got mean and angry then and began to threaten me. I found out then that I'd told him too much about myself. That first night when we talked so long, I'd told him I left Germany to escape the Kaiser's army, and how glad I am to be in America, though I mean to go back and visit my mother when the war is over. I talked very free. Well, yesterday when I told him he'd have to leave, he got real mean. He said he could fix it so I'd have to go back now. He would get me deported back to Germany and I'd be conscripted into the army and, well—"

Karl made a motion of despair and was silent. He sat with his head in his hands looking completely miserable.

"You let him scare you with a silly threat like that?" Papa spoke contemptuously. "Why, that's small-time blackmail. He wouldn't have got away with it—you only six months away from final citizenship papers! I gave you credit for better sense!"

"Is that what it's called—blackmail?" Sidney asked with interest. "Well, then that's what he was using on us, too, or trying to anyway. He said if we told on him—about the beavers, you know—and he got caught, why he'd come back and burn our barn down. And this time he'd really mean to do it. It wouldn't be an accident from smoking like last night. So you see, he even admitted starting that fire. That's what I kept telling you...."

Papa looked troubled. "Yes, I understand that now," he said. "I have apologized to Mr. Hanna, and I do so again." He glanced at the peddler, who sat quietly listening.

"But Pete Marlin will be punished, you can be sure of that—if he hasn't been already." Papa peered out through a tiny open corner in the snow-plastered window. "What I mean is that anyone out there now is in danger for his very life. If he left the shack, he's in trouble."

He stood irresolute for a few moments. "I'll try the telephone first. May be the best way to save him is to notify those along the road he's taking."

"Hello! Hello!" he called urgently, when he got the connection after repeated ringing at last. He shouted into the mouthpiece, telling the operator where the trapper was headed. "Central! Call the sheriff and tell him to get out a search party to the Marine Landing road as soon as possible. That's where he was headed from here."

The operator at Central answered that she would try, but that lines were going down fast; many were down already. Her faint voice died suddenly. There was complete silence, and now their own line was down too.

Papa looked grim. "It'll be more or less hopeless, I guess,

with phones dead. But for all we know, Pete may have gone back to the shack on the island when he saw how bad the storm was. He'd be all right there. No use endangering anyone else's life now to go looking for him. If Central gets through to the sheriff, they'll have a search party out this way soon as possible. Of course, that may not be until morning."

Those were the last words Sidney heard before numbing drowsiness overcame him. Mama, having finished giving first aid at last, had said, "I'll have supper on the table in a few minutes, soon as I get the food dished up," and he had lain back on his blanket feeling warm and at peace, and savoring the good smell of the food, but most of all the feeling of being safe and at home. He felt it really was home now.

11. Peace After the Storm

It was very late when Sidney and Elizabeth came downstairs the following morning. They had been brought upstairs and helped to bed, though neither of them had any knowledge of this. They had been too deeply asleep. Now they felt achy and hungry and out of sorts.

Calm had settled over everything; the storm was over. The experience of the evening before might almost have been a drawn-out dream, but the condition of the kitchen clearly showed its reality. It was in a state of disorder, and with gray snow still clinging to the windows and keeping out the light, it seemed dark and cheerless. Piles of clothes lay in corners where they had been dropped the night before, and here and there puddles of water from melting snow spotted the floor. A huge drift lay almost against the door; with all there was to do no one had taken time to shovel a path yet. Mama was nowhere to be seen, though the twins sat in their high chairs eating their morning oatmeal.

Sidney and Elizabeth went to the windows and looked out. Never had they seen the landscape so completely overwhelmed by whiteness. The evergreens sagged like great white tents under their heavy burdens of snow. There was no road or track anywhere. The whole landscape was a white sea. In this sea, the barn, its frame at one end blackened and broken, stood like a derelict vessel that had somehow managed to remain afloat.

Many questions raced through Sidney's mind. Mostly he wondered about Pete Marlin, the trapper. Had they found him, he wondered? Or was he lying out there somewhere, his body making a rounded bulge under the snow, like the young calf lost just before the spring snowstorm last March? Better not think about it; the picture was too grim.

Mama came in from the pantry, closing the door behind her. "Oh, you're up," she said. "I thought maybe you'd be sleeping until noon. I'll warm up the oatmeal and fix some eggs. You must be very hungry, falling asleep before supper as you did last night."

She shook up the stove and pushed in more wood. "Everything's frozen in the pantry, even the milk. I guess you'll have to drink coffee for breakfast."

They did not mind that in the least. Coffee was a great treat. They watched hungrily as the eggs sizzled in the pan, and quickly devoured the big bowls of oatmeal set before them.

Mama poured herself a cup of coffee and sat down at the table with them. She sipped silently a few minutes, watching them eat.

"I suppose you're wondering about Pete Marlin," she began. "He's all right—more than a little frozen, in the feet especially, but alive and safe. He might so easily be dead!"

"Please go on," urged Sidney eagerly. "Tell us everything. How do you know about him? Did the search party—? Where was he?"

"Near Larsen's barn. He'd gotten that far, loaded sled and all. He'd dug himself into the straw stack, just enough to keep from freezing to death. But he was found just in time—a little longer and it might be a different story. Karl found out when he went over there to do the chores for the horses a while ago. You know Mrs. Larsen was alone all night, so the cows didn't get milked, so he did that for her, too. No telling when her husband and Larry will get back through these roads."

"Oh," said Sidney, slightly disappointed. "I thought it might have been Larry who found Pete. I know it couldn't have been his mother; she hates to go out in any kind of bad weather. You can see that when she hadn't even tried to milk the cows. Was it the search party?"

"No," said Mama, pausing a moment to make her announcement more dramatic. "It was the Laugh Peddler. He both found and saved him."

The Laugh Peddler! Even the twins stared in unbelief.

"But he was here!" said Sidney. "I was just going to ask where he was. He was in this house last night—at least until I fell asleep."

"The storm let up about daybreak, and he had got up very early and left a note for us here on the table. Maybe he wasn't too comfortable sleeping on the couch. Anyway, he wrote that he was going to try to get to Larsen's to pick up his pack, and then if it was at all possible, he would try to get to Cove Pass from there and take the train home. He thought his wife would be worrying when she read about the blizzard in the morning paper, and he wanted to get home and reassure her that he was safe.

"How he made it over to Larsen's on foot, I can't imagine! Drifts are waist high in places, so you can be sure the walking was hard. But it was fortunate that he did. A few yards from the line fence he stumbled over the sled packed with furs. He knew then that Pete must be somewhere near, and he began searching around for him. And—well, that's how he found him."

Mama paused for breath, and Sidney and Elizabeth sat wide-eyed with admiration. Their Laugh Peddler—their jolly, dear, wonderful friend was a hero again! They had never known anyone so brave, nor had they ever heard anything to compare with the excitement of this story!

Pete Marlin was a horrid, wicked man, the killer of their beavers, and usurper of their island shack. He had scared them half to death and caused the barn fire and threatened blackmail. They just hoped he would be punished for all these sins. But they would not have wanted him to freeze to death in that horrible storm.

"Tell us more—tell us everything," begged Elizabeth. "Was he frozen so he couldn't walk? Did the Laugh Peddler have to carry him to the house? And what does Pete Marlin say now? I bet he's sorry he was so mean! He scared me the awfullest I've ever been scared. Will he go to jail now?"

"One question at a time, please! And look at my bread; it's rising right out of the pan, and I sit here talking!"

Mama got up quickly and took out the baking board. Then she lifted the big pan of rising dough down from the top of the stove and began to work in great handfuls of flour. She continued her story as she worked the dough.

"Our sled came in handy. Mr. Hanna could hardly have got Pete in without it. By this time the poor man was too stiff and numb to move. He couldn't even think for himself; freezing persons get drowsy, you know. So the peddler dumped out the load of furs and somehow managed to pull Pete onto the sled. That way he was able to pull him to the house. Mrs. Larsen was asleep, but he pounded on the door and she woke up. Between them, they rubbed Pete's frostbitten limbs and gave him hot drinks, and somehow they brought him to."

She gave a final strong twist to the huge mass of dough, pulling it out of the pan and onto the board, then began kneading with firm, hard punches.

"As to what Pete says now—well, the poor man is so glad just to be alive that he's confessed to everything. He admitted sleeping in our barn and starting the fire accidentally when he went to sleep that night with a cigarette. And he told how he'd threatened Karl to keep him from giving away his secret. It was just the way Karl told it. He couldn't deny killing the beavers; the skins were right there out in the snow drift. But, poor man, he's sorry about everything now, especially the way he threatened you. He said he really didn't mean to scare you so bad—just wanted to get rid of you so he could make his getaway."

"I bet he got kind of scared himself, when they told him he'd have to go to jail," Sidney smiled.

"Poor homeless man that he is—with no one caring about him one way or the other—he doesn't seem to mind. Karl said he seemed almost glad when the sheriff came for him. When you've faced death as he did, I guess you're ready to accept anything that comes with living—even jail!

"Anyway, when Sheriff told Pete where he'd be going as soon as he got out of the hospital, he said, 'Jail warm place, eh?' And when he was told that it was, he laughed and said, 'I not mind! Been cold long time, need warm-up and rest. I go to jail!' "

"Then he'll never come back and burn our barn?" Elizabeth spoke with a grateful sigh of relief.

"Oh, my no!" her mother said briskly. "He's cured of any such ideas, I'm sure. And I don't think he ever really meant that threat, either. He wasn't really such a bad man, you know. It's just that he felt he'd worked for too little pay all summer and fall, and he wanted to get even, I suppose. He felt he had something coming from this area, and so he did that terrible thing to the beavers. People who feel themselves badly treated have a way of taking it out in wrong ways."

Mama put the pan with the punched-down dough back on top of the stove and moved aside the bread board to wash dishes. "The blizzard taught him a lesson that he probably would not have learned any other way. What good were the beaver skins to him when he was in danger of freezing to death? He'll remember that, I think, and from now on he'll be careful to stay inside the law."

"Who gets the beaver skins?" asked Sidney of Papa, who had come in with a great rush of icy air. He stood slapping his arms across his chest as he always did when he was very cold. He busied himself for some moments pulling off mittens, overshoes, and outer clothing.

"I see Mama has told you the story," he said. "Well, of course the state confiscates the furs. In fact, it's already been done; the game warden was called by the sheriff. I just now talked to him up at the highway. We have the road open as far as the mailbox, and the highway crew is breaking through up there. The warden says the skins will bring a good price, with beaver so scarce. Most of it down here comes from Canada now. Wherever the skins are sold, the state will get the money."

He held out a small badge. "Wold just deputized me to be his assistant game warden. Says the territory is too big for him to get around, and from now on I'm to patrol the state land across the lake, and the island of course. That means keeping watch on what's left of the beaver colony. I can manage it during winter months when work slackens off."

Everyone admired the badge. Each twin was allowed to hold it. But Papa still could not forget the slaughtered beavers and looked unhappy.

"It's going to take years to get over this disaster," he said. "Just when the colony was beginning to thrive so well— now nearly wiped out! I see red when I think about it. But from now on, those beavers are going to be watched over like babies; that's a promise. They're going to have the best protection any wild creatures ever had. Such a thing will never happen again!"

Remembering the rows of skins they had seen strung along the wire outside the shack, Sidney wondered if there were any beavers left.

"Not many, I'm afraid," said Papa sadly. "But it was a fairly large colony, and fortunately Pete had not been at the trapping more than a couple of weeks. If he'd had longer, he might well have succeeded in killing them all off.

"Beavers, being such intelligent animals, show a kind of organization and management in emergencies that is almost human. They don't panic and run off, leaving the little ones to starve, as some animals do. No, they get more cautious, but they stay on, in spite of danger. Their instinct makes them try to save the colony from complete disaster. In fact, from what I've read, they work harder than ever to make up for their losses. Even the orphaned babies—the kits—are taken over and cared for by older brothers and sisters or those in neighboring lodges—much as good people do when small children are orphaned."

Mama spoke up briskly to close the subject. "Well, God be praised that all is as well as it is! My, what we have seen in this home in these last three days! But everything could have been so much worse, I'm thinking. Things are not so bad if even the beaver colony will survive."

Papa went to the window and looked out. The young apple trees stuck up like twigs in the drifted-high orchard. Doogan was following a small rabbit track that wound in and out, though it cost him enormous effort to leap through the deep drifts. Papa watched him idly, but his mind seemed far away.

"I treated the peddler very badly," he said softly. "I wouldn't listen to his explanation or give him a chance to defend himself about the fire. I regretted that even before last night—before I knew the real truth. I don't know what makes me be so unreasonable at times. I'm like Doogan, sniffing that rabbit trail. If he met up with a live rabbit in the snow, he probably wouldn't even want to catch him and kill him. I've kept sniffing at the peddler, bothering him all kinds of ways and cutting him down. And all the time he was—such a good, brave man."

Mama was wrapping her tie-shawl around her, preparing to go into the pantry. As she went, she closed the door carefully to keep the cold out.

Sidney moved close to Papa and, lowering his voice, began explaining about the combs. He told him that the Laugh Peddler had left them in the doll basket the day before, so they had their present for Mama, after all. That, too, showed what a good man he was, because he was faithful to a promise and trusted them to keep theirs. That's why they would like to make the down payment right away, so as not to seem to go back on their promise.

"I see," said Papa slowly. "And you're right, of course. You can send the dollar tomorrow. Mama has his St. Paul address somewhere. But the rest of it will have to wait a while, I'm afraid. I can't see my way to help you with even a small bit of money now. I don't have a dollar in my pocket since I paid for the lumber yesterday. We'll have to get along somehow until the next milk check. But we'll make out all right; we always have before. And sooner or later, we'll pay off those combs too."

He smiled a bit sheepishly. "Anyway, when you send the dollar, you'd better tell the Laugh Peddler he should come around here more often. That might keep me from getting so unreasonably cranky at times. He's got a real good way of looking at things. Whatever he sells to us, he gives us much more. I see that now. Tell him so."

12. The Shack Revisited

Sidney and Elizabeth were back just about where they'd started. They had the down payment for the combs, but nothing more, and no promise of getting anything more very soon, what with the way things were.

Because of the snow-blocked roads, there was no school. Papa said Sidney might go over to Larsen's and bring back the sled. They needed it for several things. "I'll be over a little later," he said, "but we have to have the sled right away to haul water to the stock, so don't stay long."

Sidney started off across the fields on his skis. It was the shortest way to the Larsen place. If he saw Mr. Larsen, he thought he might drop a hint that he was available for work on Saturdays. From what Larry had said, they'd be needing extra help with the fanning. Their farm was large and they did not have a steady hired man except in summer.

Sidney could not keep from looking off at the lake and the lakeshore woods, the scene of last evening's struggle. How peaceful everything was now in the brilliant morning sun! It was a different world from the one of whirling fury he had known so recently.

He stopped for a few moments, realizing suddenly how beautiful the land looked in its all-white, completely changed from the summer's green and gold. These wide spaces had a beauty that even the city he had dearly loved did not have. And when he had first come, it was those very wide spaces that had frightened him. They had seemed hostile and unconquerable. Now he had not only lost his fear, he saw quite clearly that he was coming to love the country.

Maybe it was because he felt he had become a part of it at last. The battle with the storm seemed to have proved once and for all that the new environment was not unconquerable; it could be handled if he used his head and his heart. The lost, rootless phase in his life was over, and he knew he belonged. That awareness had first come last night, with Papa's words of praise and his calling him "son."

Somewhere in these fields and woods his early childhood and his sorrow for his lost parents had been left behind. There was a more important struggle ahead, and it needed all his effort. A farm was no easy place for a city boy, but this was his place now and he would handle it.

He would never forget Daddy and Mummy. It was they who had taught him that hardship and hurt were a part of growing up, only he had not known any real ones then.

In the talk he'd had with the Laugh Peddler last spring, it had been explained best. "You have to let some things go if you are to be able to go on in a new life, but you can still hold on to them inside."

Sidney recalled his errand. But first, why not a quick trip over to the island, to check on the beavers for Papa? If he could just bring back word that he'd seen a few signs of life around the lodges in the channel, he could picture the pleased expression that would come over Papa's face. It would be worth the extra time it would take; he could still get to Larsen's and back home within an hour.

He turned, going diagonally across the field in the direction of the lake. Soon he was skirting the birch copse, then striding onto the evenly packed snow of the lake. As he went he made up his mind that he would take a careful look at everything now that there was nothing to fear. He might even find his lost jackknife, though he supposed most likely Pete would have taken it.

He strode through the dark woods of the island, pushing away the overhanging boughs of the pines that showered him with loose snow as he brushed against them. Nothing moved or stirred except his own figure, and he moved ever more slowly as the drifted-in trail led him through thorny underbrush sticking up through the snow.

Emerging from the woods, he came upon the cabin site

suddenly. He stood still with shocked surprise. All that remained of the shack were a few blackened board ends sticking out forlornly from under the drifted snow. The whole shack was burned to the ground; even the ashes were buried under the snow.

Sidney stared dazedly at the scene. He could not take in the situation at once. The shack—built piece by piece by him and Larry—was completely gone. The truth dawned slowly: Pete Marlin must have done it. He must have set it afire before he left with the furs last night, his way of destroying the evidence of illegal trapping.

"Yessir," said Sidney aloud to himself, "that must be the answer. Pete did it to destroy evidence."

Sidney's ski struck something hard in the snow—a kerosene can. That told more of the story. The trapper had sprinkled kerosene over everything and then struck a match. The wood, being old and dry, would burn easily in this sheltered spot, even in a rising snow storm.

Sidney unstrapped his skis and walked around slowly. He was conscious of a feeling of disappointment. Not only was their shack, put up with so much labor, completely destroyed, but there was nothing whatever to show now of their fantastic adventure. He had intended, after telling the boys at school the whole story, to bring them here and show them everything.

"Here, on this wire," he would say, "was where the skins were strung up—rows of them! And here inside—this big stump with the board on top—this was his skinning table. It had two big bloody knives on it. And here's where Liz'beth and I were standing when Pete Marlin sneaked in on us."

There was nothing to show now but charred ruins. Even the big stump was more than half burned. Sidney searched around in the rubble, hoping to find some small object left behind. But there was nothing left. He would not even have a small souvenir of the adventure.

The stump was still smoking inside. It had evidently been thoroughly saturated with kerosene. The snow around the thick roots was melted in a wide circle. Sidney kicked crossly at the whole blackened mass and was surprised to feel it move slightly. He put his hand on the stump, and it felt warm even through his mitten. "It must have been some fire," he mused.

He continued kicking at the charred stump, just to see how much of it he could loosen. Chunks of cindery black wood began crumbling under the kicks, and suddenly a large piece of root section broke away completely. It left a good-sized hole and exposed black, unfrozen earth. Sidney kicked away the last of the root fragments, and suddenly his foot kicked against something hard. He knelt down and clawed deeper in the dirt with his fingers, feeling something metallic. Thinking it might be a knife, he began scratching away dirt like a gopher.

Soon he had exposed a heavily rusted tin box about a foot long. He picked it up and held it in his hands a few moments, almost afraid to open it. Then, the rusty hinges creaking faintly, he managed to pull it open. A loud, trembling sigh escaped him as he stared down at its contents—a hoard of tarnished coins!

A piece of stiff brown paper lay on top, and on it, in an old-fashioned, still legible script, he read: "This is the property of Arne Nord, Marine Landing, Minn."

"The treasure!" he whispered. "I've found the money box—that Pa told about! It wasn't stolen at all. It was here all the time!"

So the story had really been true. Arne Nord *had* hidden his money on the island before he went to war, as old Eric had believed. And as Sidney had reasoned that first night after hearing the story, it was a good hiding place. All these years the money had lain there waiting to be discovered.

Sidney's mind filled with one perplexing question after another. Who had cut down the tree that sheltered the treasure, and why? Quite recently, it appeared, someone was following a clue and was warm. But who? And why had he not finished, following his hunch through to the end? From the size of the stump, it had obviously been one of the largest trees on the island. When he and Larry built the shack, they had pondered the reason for the stump when all the other trees were uncut. It had perplexed Pa, too, when he heard about it and it was what had made him remember the old treasure story.

The size and location of the tree must have made it the natural place for burying treasure. The largest pine, located in the very center of the island—why, it could hardly have been more simple.

But why then had Arne's brother not dug it up? He must have known about it, according to Pa's story. Why couldn't he find it? Why in the world would such an amount of money be left in the ground so long? And who had cut the tree down? Round and round in his mind went the questions.

Well, it didn't really matter now. The money was found —and he was the one who found it! What a story this would be to tell!

He began trembling with excitement at the thought of all the possibilities the finding of the money had opened up. He let a handful of coins sift through his fingers. "It's more

money than many people ever see in a whole lifetime," he said softly to himself. "And I'm holding it all in my hands."

Suddenly he felt uneasy and looked around fearfully. He thought of *Treasure Island* again, where near the end of the book a skeleton is found under a big pine, arms pointing toward the rifled treasure ground. It seemed almost possible that there might be something equally sinister here.

But there were no pirates here, and this was no tropical landscape. He held the money box, and nothing disturbed the serene quiet. The island floated in a world of cold white silence in which only his own figure moved.

He looked into the box again. "There must be hundreds of dollars here!" he murmured. He rubbed a coin on his mackinaw sleeve, and the tarnish cleared just enough to reveal the imprint and faint numerals. It was a twenty-dollar gold piece!

"A double eagle!" Sidney spoke aloud with awe. "And there must be dozens just of those alone!"

He examined more of the coins. The very small ones, which he had at first taken for pennies, were "half fives" or "quarter eagles." He had seen some of them before; his father had received one occasionally and had shown it to him, explaining that they were becoming valuable.

And there were three Indian Princesses. According to the Laugh Peddler, who owned one of these coins, they were very valuable. Worth three dollars at face value, they would bring much more from a collector, because there were so few of them. They were, he had explained, "a rare minting."

He was holding a fortune in his hands—the fortune Arne Nord had made more than fifty years ago from furs and fur trading. Sidney thought it sad that Arne—and his brother too—should have died without ever having any good of the money. But, never having known either of them, he could not be too unhappy about that. He could only feel elation that he had been the one lucky enough to find it.

He began strapping on his skis with trembling hands. If he did not tell someone about this immediately, he was afraid he would burst with excitement.

Grand dreams raced through his head as he skied back across the snow-covered lake, clutching the money box. The Miller financial troubles were all over now. Many, many things, impossible even to think of before, would be easily attainable with all this money!

Suddenly the rhinestone combs became only a small trifle. With this money Mama would be able to choose anything she wanted from the Laugh Peddler's pack or from any store. She and Elizabeth could have yards and yards of lace now. Why, they could have lace on everything they wore!

And Pa would have the new plow he needed—a riding plow like those most good farmers had. They were the thing now; one-horse walking plows were for "small farmers" only. And there would be a cream separator so they could sell cream instead of milk. With butterfat so high, it paid much better to sell cream. Oh, now at last they would catch up with the best of farmers around here!

Elizabeth—his heart leaped at the thought of what the money would buy for her. She should have the doll bed and dresser that she had told him she wanted last Christmas but had not found under the tree. Until this moment he knew there was no chance she'd get them this Christmas either. But now—why, he could go to the Company Store and buy anything, just like that!

The twins should have a riot of toys, like two-year-old babies ought to have, instead of just home-made spool rattles and stocking dolls. Yes, even Karl should have some luxuries to cheer his hard-working life. After all, he had not been to blame for any of Pete Marlin's wrongdoing.

And he himself—well, why shouldn't he have a Flexible Flyer sled now? Maybe next summer even a bicycle! He and Larry could go all kinds of places together then.

And—Sidney's eyes fairly danced at the thought—they might even get an automobile! Only a few people, mostly "big farmers," had motorcars now, and very proud they were, too, of their "machines." They talked their automotive jargon even at Farmers' Club meetings, making the others very conscious that they were still "horse and buggy."

No reason now why Pa should not get one too! It might have to be a car for country roads, small and light like the Model T Ford that some folks called "puddle jumpers" because they could get through muddy roads where larger, heavier cars bogged down hopelessly. With an automobile, they would be freed from the chore of having to hitch up horses every time they wanted to go somewhere.

Perhaps by spring they would be driving their own car! He could picture Pa at the wheel with driving goggles and gloves, and Mama beside him in a long dust coat, with a protective veil swathed over her hat.

Sidney felt quite intoxicated with his extravagant plans. He seemed to move in a dream—a too-good-to-be-true dream. But it *was* true! He had the hard, solid feel of the money box in his hand to prove it.

Now and then he could not help letting out an exuberant shout into the wide, white stillness. He was simply too elated to be able to keep still, and it was taking too long to get home.

13. The Treasure Is Returned

Sidney's heart was pounding like a hammer as he turned up from the lake toward the farmyard and the house. He could see Papa at work between the barn and the granary. He was shoveling snow, and only his head and shoulders showed above the great bank of snow he had already raised with his shovel.

Sidney skied up to him panting. "I've found it!" he blurted out happily. "I've got the money box from the island!" He forgot everything he had planned to say and just held out the box.

"Yes, what have you got?" asked Papa a bit crossly, not even looking up from his shoveling. "I saw you coming there on the lake, and I could see you didn't have the sled that you were supposed to go over to Larsen's and bring back. Did you forget I said I needed it right away—to haul water to the sheep and stock?"

"But I've got the treasure! I found Arne Nord's money box—see!" Sidney glided down into the trench and opened the box in front of Papa's face. He began to sift the coins through his fingers.

Papa's eyes widened and his mouth fell open. The shovel slid out of his hands and fell softly into the snow. He stood silent, staring as if he had seen a ghost.

"What are you saying?" he stammered at last. "What— where—? I don't believe it! It's impossible!"

Sidney laughed delightedly. This was as good as any of the Laugh Peddler's jokes. The expression on Pa's face!

"But it *is* true," he said. "I found it a little while ago under that big stump I told you about on the island. The shack's been burned down; I guess Pete Marlin did it to destroy the evidence of killing the beavers. There's nothing left but ashes and ruins. But the stump was still smoking inside, and I kicked at it, and some pieces of the roots broke off. A real big piece came off and the dirt showed under it, and I was kicking in it and felt something hard. So I scratched around and dug it up and well, it was the box—the money box. See, it even has his name in it."

Papa sat down right in the soft snow, took off his mittens, and took the box in his hands. He peered closely at it and said, "Begin at the beginning. Tell the whole thing— how you found it. I still can't quite take it in somehow."

So Sidney told his story again, this time from the beginning. He explained how he had meant to make the detour to the island just to see if he could find any beavers. "I thought it would cheer you up, you know, if I saw even one or two...."

He described the burned-down shack once more and the smoking stump, the kicking at burned-off bits of root until he kicked at the box. "It was in kind of solid, so I had to pull at it hard to get it out. I brushed off the dirt and well, that's it. That's the whole story."

Papa began picking up the coins and studying them. As if speaking to himself, he said slowly. "I still can't believe it! I only half believed that story, you know. And all the time it was true! Poor Arne Nord—saving his money and hiding it so well, then having no good of it whatsoever."

He appraised some of the coins tentatively. "This is not only money, you see. It's valuable money because it's so old. Most of the coins are worth more than their face value. It's almost a small fortune—will be to them anyway."

He became suddenly brisk and purposeful. "We must call up to John Nord's right away. He's Arne's nephew, you know—old Jonas Nord's son. As far as I know, he'll be the only heir. The money is his, so we must give him the good news right away. Oh, I tell you he'll be glad!" He turned quickly and began striding toward the house.

Suddenly everything appeared completely gray and bleak to Sidney. His wonderful dreams! They had collapsed with a crash. The money would not even be theirs!

The Treasure Is Returned

In stories he read, treasure always went to the finders. Look at *Treasure Island*—how well Jim Hawkins ended up. And from beginning to end almost, this had seemed like a storybook adventure. But the ending was spoiled now for him.

Some parts of Papa's story came back to him now. The John Nord who'd had the corn-binder accident had been mentioned, but Sidney had attached little importance to the fact at the time, intrigued as he was with the story of the treasure itself. Naturally, this John Nord, being a nephew of the man who buried the money, would be his heir. What a stupid mistake to forget that! It was about the only fact in the whole story that he had forgotten, but it was the most important one.

Sidney stood silent and crestfallen for several minutes. He unstrapped his skis slowly. Let Pa tell the story and get the excitement over with, since the money would not be theirs anyway.

"My big ideas!" he snorted, blowing his nose hard. "As if I could ever get to keep such a treasure—even if I found it!" He stood the skis against the side of the woodshed and went into the house.

As he opened the kitchen door, Mama and Elizabeth looked up eagerly. "Wonderful, Sidney!" they cried, and Mama added glowingly, "Oh, what a good thing for the Nords!"

They, with Papa, were bending over the coins spread on the kitchen table. Papa had stacked the coins in piles and was completing the counting. "Close to a thousand dollars, as near as I can figure in a hurried count. I get $965, but with the tarnish I may have misread a few. That's a nice round sum in itself, but some of the coins are worth much more than face value. It's hard to say just how much they will bring. This is money made from beaver skins—you can be sure of that. The greediest slaughter went on seventy-five to a hundred years ago; it's what made beavers nearly extinct."

He paused, remembering the recent killing of the island beavers. "But this money comes to a good end, anyway. It will do plenty for that family. The bad luck they've had! His hurt leg—how he's suffered with that, and the debts he's had to get into because of the accident. If anyone can use a windfall like this, they can!"

"Oh, how good that you found it, Sidney!" said Mama again. She looked over at him lovingly as he stood near the door. He took off his outer clothes and hung them up.

"Lucky the telephone lines are fixed," said Papa, going into the dining room and cranking the handle. "Ring John Nord's place over by Four Corners, Central," he said. "I have some good news for him." He stood smiling into the mouthpiece.

In spite of his disappointment, Sidney began to feel a small enjoyment in the situation. It was exciting just to listen to the one-sided conversation that followed when Central got John Nord on the line. Mama even left her baking to come in and listen.

Papa began by saying he had some good news for him, and then after a short pause, he related the story of the finding of the money box, straight through from the beginning. He explained how the children had discovered Pete Marlin's hideout on the island the day before, and how Pete had been trapping beavers. He told how Sidney went back this morning on an impulse, and how he found the shack burned down. When he came to the climax—the finding of the money box under the smoldering stump—Sidney's heart began thumping wildly. He relived the discovery all over again. It really was an adventure story—the best imaginable —no matter how the money part ended.

Papa told it excitingly, too, but he had to keep repeating some things over and over. It appeared that John Nord was simply unable to believe the story. He found it just too good to be true.

"Yes, we have the money right here," or "Yes, it was under the big pine all those years. Someone had sawed it down and it was a big stump now."

After a while, Papa stopped talking and stood listening, his eyes bright with interest. It was clear that John Nord had a story to tell, too, and now that his first surprise was over, he was filling in the missing details.

"I see," and "Oh, that's why," and other responses Papa was making had them all wild with curiosity. Finally, Papa said heartily, "Yes, yes, come over as soon as you can. We have the money here. It's right in the kitchen waiting for you."

The Treasure Is Returned

After he had hung up, he groaned, "Whew! That wasn't easy! I didn't know it would be so hard to convince a man he's become suddenly rich. Poor fellow, he's had such a hard time making out these last months, and had so much bad luck, now he just can't believe in a bit of good news. But he will when he sees the money."

"What else did he say?" asked Sidney excitedly. "Did he say why they never found it—his father or him—all those years? They must have looked for it. And does he know who cut the tree down?"

"Just a minute—one question at a time!" Papa mopped his brow in mock exasperation, but anyone could see that he was really enjoying himself. He added the final touches to the story that had been a mystery for such a long time.

"Well, to begin with, John doesn't remember his uncle. He was a baby when Arne Nord went to war. But he does remember as a small boy going with his father to dig for the money. It was always done in secret because his father feared robbery in case they would actually find the money box. But they were never able to locate it.

"When Arne, in that southern prison camp, knew that he wasn't going to make it back, he wrote to his brother Jonas, willing him all his possessions—and that was chiefly the money box buried on the island. He gave directions for finding it. Well, those directions were to 'measure off 80 paces from the east shore inlet, then 10 paces to the right until you come to the good-sized pine at the center of the island. It's the largest of the pines in that spot.'

"John says he and his father found five trees that would fit that description. Maybe the inlet was a small place then, but now it's wide, and they weren't able to decide what was the exact spot to begin the pacing off. Anyway there were five 'good-sized pines' at the center of the island. Trees are like people; some grow fast and some slow, so the trees that were smaller when he buried the money box might have overtaken the original biggest pine later. Anyway, they couldn't decide which was the right one, and so they dug under them all, but without success. Jonas had done some digging by himself, too, in the earlier years; he was positive it was the tallest pine tree, and he dug there over and over.

"After several more tries, he concluded that the money must have been stolen soon after it was buried. He died suspicious of some of his neighbors. But John somehow never could stop thinking about that box, and he made up his mind to try again—using his head as well as his back, you might say.

"He figured that the 'good-sized pine' might be the one that was widest around. So he brought a tapeline and began measuring the five trees, and he found one was several inches wider than the rest, showing it was older and might have been the biggest years ago. He figured that must be the one, but the roots were so big and tangled near the surface, it was impossible to dig around it much, so he decided the thing to do was cut it down. So he and his oldest boy sawed it down more than a year ago—secretly of course, since you have no right to cut trees on state land. They went in from the other side of the lake and crossed over the ice at the channel—where the beaver houses are. He figured the stump would rot after a while or they would burn it out, using kerosene, you know.

"Well, they went over to do that this past summer, but then they found your shack built right over it and, with the boy along and all, he didn't have the heart to burn the place down. He decided to hold off a little longer until you abandoned the shack—maybe this fall. When they came home, the boy was full of talk about the shack on the island and the beaver houses they'd seen in the channel. They had a hired man at the time; I think you can guess who it was."

"Pete Marlin!" exclaimed Sidney. "That's how he knew!"

"Correct. And I guess you know the rest of the story. Early in September John Nord had the corn-binder accident. He's hardly been able to walk these three months. And for all they've spent on doctors around here, his leg isn't getting any better. His wife and the older boy do the work, and they have three younger children—one a baby. So you know this money will be a godsend to them! The doctors here say he needs an operation by specialists to fix up the leg, and now he can go to Rochester and have it done."

Mama beamed with pleasure. "Oh, my, how good!" she said softly. Tears shone in her eyes as she returned to her work in the kitchen.

Papa turned to Sidney. "Yes, it *is* good," he said with a

wry smile. "And if you'd gone straight over to Larsen's instead of making that detour to the island, who knows when that money would have been found—if ever? Sometimes a bit of willfulness will accomplish what plans over many years have failed to do."

Then, lest Sidney should think he was condoning all kinds of willful disobedience, he added, "God moves in a mysterious way His wonders to perform." But he stroked Sidney's hair as he said it.

The gesture moved Sidney to a sudden confidence. "But I thought the money would be mine!" he blurted out. "I found it, and I never remembered about John Nord at all. I thought 'finders, keepers,' you know—the way it is in books. It was a big disappointment," he added lamely. "I wanted to give the money to you—to show you...."

"Yes, what was it you wanted to show?" asked Papa gently.

"That I could—well, do something nice for you to sort of pay you back for taking me in—giving me a home so I didn't have to go to the orphanage. I know you're hard up, and I'm not good at helping with farmwork like Karl—at least not yet. I just wanted to—I thought this would prove—"

Papa put an arm around Sidney's thin shoulders and looked into his face. "You don't need to prove anything—except maybe that you like us enough to want to go on living with us. It hasn't been easy for you, Son, I know. I haven't done what I should to help you, either. But this has been a tough year; nothing has gone right on the farm, and then I get grouchy and short-tempered. But that doesn't mean—I didn't mean to take it out on you. Why, you're our boy! We've taken out papers to adopt you, so you know we've wanted you right from the beginning."

"Then I'll really belong to this family?" Sidney's eyes shone.

"Yes, indeed. To this family, such as we are—with plenty of trouble and never enough of some things, especially money. Not the biggest bargain as families go, but you're a part of it!"

Papa turned serious as he added, "But don't ever stop remembering your own parents—or trying to be like them. I never knew your father, but I have an idea he was a better man than I am in many ways. He had more patience and probably stood up to trouble better than I do. That's worth a lot, even if he had nothing else to leave you. Like the Laugh Peddler now—the spirit he has is worth much more than the kind of living he makes, only I was too blind to see that until last night when he risked his life to go after you in the blizzard. That kind of spirit is worth more than any treasure; don't ever forget it."

He carefully scooped the money back into the box and tied it up with cord. His eyes were almost as bright and twinkly as the Laugh Peddler's as he began dressing to go outdoors.

"John Nord and his wife will be coming over as soon as the boy gets the horses hitched up—maybe a couple of hours or so." He suddenly looked directly at Sidney, smiling mischievously. "Yes, and I completely forgot to tell you —with so much talk it went right out of my head—but there's to be a reward for the finder, John said. I shouldn't wonder if it's enough for—well, you can be sure it will be a nice tidy little sum, anyway."

Sidney and Elizabeth both let out joyful whoops. The rhinestone combs could be paid for! They would be a paid-up Christmas present after all.

Papa smiled as he bent down to put on his overshoes. "I'm going over to Larsen's to talk to him and to bring the sled back. Yusef Hanna will be gone, of course, but tomorrow when the mail comes through again, we'll send a letter with the money in it to him—to the St. Paul address. It will be a nice surprise for him."

The children nodded, glancing at the pantry door for fear Mama might suddenly return and overhear what they were saying.

"What is it he says about trouble now?" asked Papa innocently. "Something about 'a long face,' isn't it?"

"A long face lengthens your troubles. A laugh puts them out of sight!" chanted Sidney and Elizabeth in unison.

"Well, he has a pretty good idea there," said Papa, opening the door to let in a great rush of cold air. "We must try to remember it a little more often."

Mama looked questioningly at the smiling faces as she came back from the pantry. She untied her shawl and set down a big basket of apples.

"I was keeping these for pies," she said. "But just look

how frozen they are! They'll begin to shrivel right away. Only the ones on the bottom can be saved, I'm afraid; the rest will have to go to the pigs. It's a good thing we put the best Wealthies upstairs. At least we'll have some eating apples for Christmas."

She brought out the lamps and began to wash the sooty chimneys briskly. "Elizabeth, you amuse the twins now; they're already tired of their high chairs. And you bring in some wood, Sidney. Bring both stove lengths and a few split chunks for the heater. We want to have it warm in the dining room when the Nords come. Maybe they'll be staying for dinner."

Her face was bright and happy. "I just can't take it in yet! It's such a wonderful blessing. Sometimes a thing will happen in an ordinary place like this that seems almost like a miracle. Yes, like a miracle right out of the Laugh Peddler's land! But who would ever think such a thing could happen here?" She hummed softly as she polished a lamp chimney to shining brightness, then lifted the twins down from their high chairs.

Sidney and Elizabeth looked at each other. It was quite plain that she had no idea of anything beyond the good fortune that had suddenly come to John Nord and his family. She had not the slightest inkling about the combs—that they would be hers for Christmas. That was their own private miracle—theirs and the Laugh Peddler's.

THE END

About the Author

ALICE CHRISTGAU, whose memories of her childhood home in Minnesota, are so warmly recorded in her two books, *Runaway to Glory* and *Rosabel's Secret*, has now written a third book set in the same area. The new story is about a peddler who traveled from farm to farm in the early 1900's. "Peddlers were quite common when I was a child," Mrs. Christgau notes, "and the character, Yusef Hanna, is drawn from my remembrance of a jolly, lovable peddler who often came to our door."

Mrs. Christgau, a mother of three grown children, taught for several years and wrote for magazines before launching into her book-writing career. She and her husband now live in Oakland, California.

About the Artist

ARVIS STEWART grew up on a farm in North Texas and was graduated from Texas Technological College in Lubbock with a bachelor's degree in Advertising Art and Design. His own personal memories of the joys as well as the heartaches of living on a farm are reflected in his highly imaginative illustrations for *The Laugh Peddler*.

Mr. Stewart and his wife, who is also a freelance illustrator, live in New York City.